THE EDGE

Also by Page Stegner:

ESCAPE INTO AESTHETICS: The Art of Vladimir Nabokov

a novel by Page Stegner

THE EDGE

THE DIAL PRESS, INC.   1967
NEW YORK

ACKNOWLEDGMENTS

"Sunday Morning" by Wallace Stevens: Copyright 1923 and renewed 1951 by Wallace Stevens. Reprinted from *Collected Poems of Wallace Stevens* by permission of Alfred A. Knopf, Inc. and Faber and Faber Limited.

"The Double Axe" by Robinson Jeffers: From *The Double Axe and Other Poems* by Robinson Jeffers. Copyright 1947, 1948 by Robinson Jeffers. Reprinted by permission of Random House, Inc.

"Night" by Robinson Jeffers: Copyright 1925 and renewed 1953 by Robinson Jeffers. Reprinted from *Selected Poetry of Robinson Jeffers* by permission of Random House, Inc.

"The Song of Wandering Aengus" by William Butler Yeats: Reprinted with permission of The Macmillan Company from *Collected Poems* by William Butler Yeats. Copyright 1906 by The Macmillan Company, renewed 1934 by William B. Yeats. Reprinted by permission of Mr. M. B. Yeats and Macmillan & Co., Ltd., London.

"Love for Sale" by Cole Porter: Copyright 1930 by Harms, Inc.

"Jimmy Brown the Newsboy" by A. P. Carter: Copyright 1931 Peer International Corporation. Copyright renewed Peer International Corporation. Used by permission.

Printed in the United States of America   First printing, 1968
Design by Lynn Hatfield

FOR MARION

Prologue

π The boy woke when the first smoky light began to penetrate the cabin. At first he did not know where he was. At home his curtains were pale yellow and they were the first thing he saw every morning, but here the curtains were a heavy dark red. When he sat up to try to place himself they paled and then brightened as the first rays of sun shot bloody streaks through their faded folds. In the dim light he could pick out huddled forms on the beds and on the floor, dark shapes shrouded in gray blankets and sleeping bags. The room smelled peculiar to him, fetid and sour, like scorched husks and wine and cigarette smoke. He slid to the bottom of the bed and swung his legs over, remembering now that he was here with his father for the weekend and that he had been promised waffles for breakfast. Easing off the bed he padded quietly across the floor to the bathroom. The window had been left open and as his bare feet touched the cold linoleum he was shocked wide

awake. Carefully raising the seat as his mother had in-
structed him to do, he used the toilet, and went back into
the overheated, stale room to find his clothes. He dressed
and quickly tiptoed around the sleepers to find his father,
but his father wasn't there.

Not there, God help me. I wasn't around. But it doesn't
matter. I know how it went. I know how he looked, just
as I know how he was bewildered when he woke up. I
know because it goes on in my head all the time. Things
happen on the world inside or in the world outside or on
no side of any world anywhere. I can't tell. But it doesn't
matter. They happen. You don't have to be front row center to know how things are. I know what he did when he
got up. I know he was frightened because he was hardly
four years old and strange people frightened him, and I
know he looked into every sleeping bag and bed where I
was not, and when he couldn't find me, he went out of the
cabin, barefooted and without his coat, onto the dusty
path that leads through nasturtiums and wild oats and
poppies down to the lodge. I see it all very clearly.

He stood a few shivering moments at the top of a slope
in the dew-wet grass beside the path and looked down
over the row of cabins just below, across the redwood
deck of the lodge below the cabins, and out over the strip
of lawn beyond the deck to the ice-plant fringe that marks
the end of land. Beyond that stretched a restless ocean
that begins, unseen from above, in rock and surf and spray
five hundred feet below the ice-plant fringe, at the bottom
of the storm-sculptured cliffs that rise from the sea. Kelp
heads bobbed and disappeared, popped up again in a
chorus-line dance, and ducked back into green-black
swells.

On his left a low bank of orange poppies cut off the coast to the south, and as he scrunched his toes in the dust he glanced over his shoulder into the rising sun, orange as a poppy itself, its radiance still diffuse behind a veil of morning fog. I know how this was too, because I have been there. I am there now. The head swims in a sea of poppies, orange on a field of orange, pinpricks of green oat, crissed but not crossed by weathered gray cedar posts that teeter and totter and fence out a collapsing time and space, and all of it in motion, swirling, pulsing upward in a maelstrom haze of green, gray, orange, red fog. I know because I looked into that same sun, on that same morning, when Dasha's erotic fumbles waked me out of a troubled sleep and I leaned across her and pulled back the curtain by her bed to peer, bleary eyed, at my opaque image in that golden glass.

Dizzy, the boy sat down in the dust and squeezed his eyes shut. The violent patterns continued, screened on purple parchment lids, crissed and crossed and watermarked. He turned his face away from the sun and opened his eyes on the sea. Kelp heads bobbed in the green-black swells. On the cliff edge he saw the orange beach ball his father had given him on the drive down from San Francisco, impaled in the spiky tongue of ice plant that licked up over the rock. He stood, thinking that he would go and get it.

Ah, miserable and accursed, if we had not stopped in that supermarket for beer, I would not have bought that ninety-nine-cent bladder of plastic that beckons my wingless Icarus with its gaudy poppycolor to the overhanging edge of the world and sends him hurtling down into a cold and green-black night. But it was not yet. Not yet. I see it before it happens. The world inside makes inadmissible jumps and must be reminded that verisimilitude is a serious business.

I see him as he started down the path toward the lodge, walking carefully to avoid the stones that bruised his bare feet. At the rickety wooden steps that led down from the upper bank he paused. An elderly woman in a tweed coat and faded dungarees was climbing up, slowly, methodically, her eyes on her feet. At the top step she nearly ran into the boy and looked up startled. "Out for an early walk," she explained hastily, as if she had been caught at some impropriety. Her remark struck her as foolish and she ran her fingers through her short gray hair and snorted.

"Goodness." She snorted again. *"You* are certainly up early. Looks like we are the only two awake around here." She looked back down the steps to confirm her observation and then added vaguely, "On this lovely morning. . . ."

"It's not *too* early," the boy said. "We're going to have waffles."

The gray lady said nothing and she continued to look absently around her as if she had lost something but couldn't remember what it was.

"My father wasn't in the cabin," the boy added.

"Where is your mother, little boy?" said the old woman. "Maybe she knows where he is."

"Not here," he replied. "She didn't come here. My father and her don't live together. They *hate* each other."

"Oh!" said the woman. Again she looked rather confounded, and then after a bit she said, "How do you know?"

The boy put one hand on the railing and the other on his hip and looked out to sea. In conversations with adults one should appear wise. "Oh, well . . ." he said, ". . . just because."

"I see," said the woman, who did not.

"My father left our gray house at the uvin . . . universiny a really long time ago and he hasn't been home for about a hundred years. Till he came to get me for the weekend." He scuffed his left foot in the dust and leaned on the rail and looked at the woman. "He's a resondible bum."

"Oh," said the lady again. "You mean . . ." and she paused, "irresponsible?"

"That's what I said," he answered. "Resondible."

"Goodness," she said. "What a way to talk about your father." She titched and snorted.

"It's what my mother says," the boy told her.

"Perhaps she's right," said the old lady. "Perhaps you better go and find him before he gets lost." And I see her standing in the center of the top step, breathing the salt air in great gulps, appropriating the soft morning mist. The boy, sensing that she was not soon going to move, turned and walked back toward the cabin.

He passed the one in which he had slept and moved on to its identical twin twenty feet down the path. Inside, under beards and blankets, amidst bras and pants and shoes and overflowing ashtrays, damp towels, and half emptied jugs of tepid wine, were more of the creatures that he and his father had come down the coast with. And in the dark jumble of sleeping figures he moved from nest to nest searching for me. But I was not there either. Not in that particular hell. Away in the mountains and valleys of Dasha the barmaid, not thinking or caring or knowing that other needs were greater than mine, I rolled my caissons over hill and dale, waded through tide pools of salty sweat, marched my troops in steaming jungles where poppies never grow. But not in that hell where he searched. Two levels up, three circles down, I don't know. But not there.

During a lull in the battle she said, "Hey! What's with the wedding ring?"

"Married once." Good eye, Dasha. First time you've noticed.

"Not now?"

"No."

"I mean, it doesn't matter to me or anything. You're divorced, huh?"

"We didn't get along."

"A new wrinkle."

Conversations in bed are also a new wrinkle. "I used to live with my mother. Couldn't stand my mother. She's a harpy. I had to get out. She worked, I went to school, we had a kid."

"Your *mother* and you?"

"No, for Christ's sakes. My wife and I. We had a kid. The longer I went to school the less I dug my wife. I sort of outgrew her, you know? So I split."

"How long you go to school?"

"Six years. To graduate school."

"Hey! You a doctor or something?"

"Nope. I quit. But I'm a master. Name is Bates. Master Bates."

"You're not very original. You going to talk all morning? Like the song says, if you can't bite, don't growl."

The boy turned in his search toward the door to an adjoining room. Behind it bedsprings squeaked rhythmically and he pulled it open and peered in, calling my name. A furtive rustle and a soft woman's voice. "Your daddy's not here, honey. Run along and play." And he went back outside, beginning to be really frightened now, thinking that his father had forgotten him. Deserted him in a wild and lonely place with strangers whom he did not like, strangers who laughed at nothing, and used words he had been told never to say; queer people who slept where they fell and ate when they pleased, who offered him brown cigarettes and howled when he asked his father what a "toke" was. In a panic he ran down the path toward the parking lot next to the lodge, ignoring the stones now because they were blurred and fluid along the track. Grass and vines and ocean and path and lodge all dissolved into a watery green-brown fingerpainting of formless shapes. But in the parking lot his father's battered yellow Ford reassured him and he climbed into its front seat to fight his tears. He put his hands on the sides of his head and pulled his eyes into tight slants to stop the water. Then he lay on the seat, pressing his face into the worn fuzz of the cushions, and put his thumb into his mouth. After a few moments he shifted his position, and then shifted it again, now on his back, plucking at the fuzz with one hand, thumb still in his mouth.

A fly buzzed against the windshield glass and finally escaped through the open wind-wing. The boy thought he heard someone crunching across the gravel of the parking lot and he stopped plucking fuzz and sat up. A moth-eaten Airedale belonging to Gina Pope, the soft voice in the squeaking room, was stiff-legging it around toward the rear of the lodge where the garbage pails were kept. The boy had played with the dog all the way down from San Francisco, even though it had growled at him and snapped once when he became too affectionate. The dog's name was Gregory Peck and he was old and had terrible breath and was not accustomed to much attention. The boy climbed out of the car and followed the ratty tail around the corner of the building. "Hey there, Gregory." Gregory stopped and waited without looking around, and the boy came up and rubbed its tufted back. From under disreputable eyebrows the dog regarded him warily for a moment and then slowly sniffed away toward the galvanized cans behind the kitchen door.

The boy watched it and then turned and walked back toward the parking lot and around to the front of the lodge. He sat on the lawn where it sloped up to the redwood deck and looked at the kelp heads ducking and weaving in the swells beyond the cliff. His orange ball was still caught in its spiny trap of ice plant, backdropped by a green-black sea. Rising to his feet he moved slowly down toward it.

In the dining room a girl is setting the tables for breakfast. She is pretty except when she opens her mouth. Her hair is long and auburn and falls straight down her shoulders. Her eyes are green and very wide and her nose is straight and thin. Her figure is splendid, almost too splendid in places, for her breasts are enormously large for her height, which is not great. They are very firm, however, and she seldom entrusts them to a bra. This, she thinks, is what makes Big Sur a groovy place to live. *Groovy* is her term for almost everything that permits her to "express" herself freely. She is a pretty, well-built girl except when she opens her mouth. There are black frames around most of her teeth.

The girl's name happens to be Martha. This morning Martha is not at her best. She is, in fact, horribly hung over and she moves slowly, trying to ignore the bowling alley in her head. As she goes from table to table, placing napkins and silverware, she carries a bottle of Coke, and she pauses frequently to water the parched deserts of her mouth and throat. She stops in front of a tinted bay window to swish stinging bubbles through her fur-lined teeth and she notices a small boy ambling across the lawn toward a bright orange ball. She sees the ball in the ice plant that borders the cliff and she sees the boy, but he moves so languidly across the soft grass, so in tune with her own semiconscious condition, that she makes no connection between the two. A perverse imp is bowling strikes just behind her left eye and as he racks up another three-hundred game the machinery breaks down. There is a short circuit in the pinsetter and a general power failure in the alley.

Martha is not at her best this morning. Her heart burns and not from love. No light-winged Dryad sings in her tree. She thinks she may puke. Her head throbs, her breasts are sore, she has bad gas. She leans on a table, Coke in one hand half raised to her mouth, and watches the boy as he pauses and bends over to pick something from between his toes. Then she puts the bottle on the window ledge and stoops to move the sugar bowls from the bottom rack of her cart to the top so that she can place them on the tables without aggravating her head by constant bending over. When she stands up she has to close her eyes and lean against the wall until the dizziness passes, and then she looks out the window again at the sea. In the few minutes that her attention has been diverted the scene has changed. The sun has burned off the last thin shroud of morning fog, the ocean is turquoise around the offshore rocks, the boy and his ball are gone. She turns and goes into the kitchen for glasses and coffee cups, thinking how swiftly the moods of the coast can change, and she comments on it to the tall, bearded cook. The cook, when not otherwise occupied, is a metal sculptor. He is also Martha's current lover and he is tortured this morning by the same affliction that is tearing up her insides. He makes no comment on her observation and does not turn around until he hears the splintering of glass on the tile floor and his lady's anguished moan. She leaves the kitchen in such a rush that he lays down the whip and the bowl of eggs that he is scrambling and follows her out into the dining room. From the window he sees her leap clumsily from the redwood deck and fly across the lawn toward the cliff, and startled he moves quickly through the porch door. He goes down the steps, taking them two at a time, but when he reaches her she is huddled back on the grass, head on her knees, hands on her head. She is hysterical and cannot tell him why, and when he looks cautiously over the precipice at the surf pounding the rocks far below he can see nothing but an orange beach ball bobbing out in the swell with the kelp heads.

I had a son once, and his name was Sonny and he fell over the western edge of the land into the sea and I could not find him though I looked everywhere and asked everybody. "Sonny," I cried. "Come on, and we'll go get those waffles I promised. All you can eat. And I have a story to tell you when we finish. About where I was and what I did."

It's like a fairy tale. You'll understand. I met a witch in a house on a cliff and she was sitting in a tub of scalding water in the dark of the moon, combing her coal-black hair. She took me in her tub and we flew through pale tunnels of moonlight down into a cavern in hell where a single flame flickered and the air was full of sulphur and naked bodies writhed in huge tanks of scalding oil and we could hear below us the hissing of sea snakes. We went down steps to a beach of red sand that moved endlessly underfoot, and all around us were cliffs of gaping mouths that came sucking at us, but they could not cross the red sand and the snakes could not come out of the water because the sand kept moving them back, endlessly, as it ran out to sea like cloth off a weaver's loom. Out on the dark red ocean I saw a huge boat, and as I watched, it broke in the middle and sank, but when I looked again it was there, sailing along, and then it broke in the middle and sank once more. On the beach there were hundreds of blue lotus leaves and we picked them until our arms were full, and each leaf was alive and writhed in our hands and wound itself around our arms and legs. On the dark red waters we watched the tigers bound. All night I struggled with this witch and when at last it was over and I had beaten her I was so exhausted that I fell down where I was and slept as if I were dead, and when I waked up everything was gone.

I asked the man in the restaurant, "Have you seen my boy?"

"Small boy?" he said. "Blond, about so high?"

"Yes," I said. "Where is he? I've lost him."

"You certainly have," he said, and went back to his frying pan.

Outside I met a waitress with auburn hair and green eyes, lying in a heap on the lawn. "Excuse me," I said. "I'm lost. That is, my boy is lost."

She looked up and smiled. "Small boy, blond?"

"Yes," I said.

"What was his name?" she asked.

"What do you mean *was*?" I shouted. "Where is he? I promised him waffles."

"Gone," she said wistfully. "Gone. Besides, waffles aren't on the menu."

I am running, running, past the cabins and through the field to the old rubber tire that hangs from an oak tree. I strike the oak's rough, corrugated hide and howl my question at its deaf ears. And I am running again, with bleeding hands, around and around the field, past the cabins, until I meet an old woman with tweed hair and a gray jacket, walking along a path. "Have you seen a small boy?" I yell at her.

"Well," she says, and looks both startled and absent. "I saw one a while back whose father was irresponsible. I suppose that's you?"

Again I am running, down the path to the lodge, past the cliff that drops off into rocks and sea and kelp, to the place where a fair-haired girl sits crumpled on the grass.

"Still looking?" She smiles secretly.

"Yes!" I shout, shaking her violently. "I'm still looking."

"Waffles aren't on the menu," she says.

"My boy is lost."

"Small boy, blond?"

"I told you before."

"Fell off the edge," she says. "Him and his ball."

For weeks and weeks I am running, riding, running, driving, through lemon groves and past beaches, down lanes of eucalyptus and white cottages. Down crowded streets, filthy with refuse and blown newspapers, through fog and smog and fog and more smog. Past billboards and shopping centers, fruit stands and standing fruits. Past burgers and shakes, fish sandwich and chips, taco bars, giant oranges, Dairy Queens and motorcycle queens. Mystery spots, caves and caverns. Until my head swells like a ripe pomegranate and pops, spilling out purple seeds that roll and twitch like jumping beans. I run and run toward a hole in the far corner of my fright and slip through it into a darkness where it is cool and the air no longer smells like fried fish, and I can see at the end of my tunnel a rectangle of light and Ellen standing inside it. I come close to her and see not pity or anger or hatred on her worn and tired face, only grief. She seems not surprised at my presence. She looks, in fact, supremely indifferent.

"Ellen," I'm shouting. "Not my fault. I was powerless. I wasn't there. *I was not even there,* I'm telling you. I couldn't do anything about what I didn't see. You're accusing me without even . . ."

"Nobody has accused you," she says in her tired voice and gently closes the door.

I stand in the hallway screaming at the apartment door. "I didn't do anything. Not one damn thing. I'm not guilty of anything. *Not guilty.*" And all of a sudden there is a terrible rip in the fabric of my darkness and I am lost again and running in the blinding light that will not shut off even when I close my eyes.

PART ONE

I

π My kennel is on the second floor. Like most of the cubicles at this level it is private, or more or less so, and I am privileged not because I have money or friends, but because the wards on the third and fourth floors are full. Besides, the doctors do not think that I will be here long.

My window looks out on a lawn about the size of a football field, covered now with snow and bordered on three sides by the ponderosa pines that grow thick on the mountains around this retreat. They are dense and black and on dank days when the clouds settle down in them they look more like stuccoed tents than pines. At certain times they frighten me, and there is a strange, morose little girl on this floor who lives in perpetual terror of those trees.

I have a work table under my window and a typewriter, and I like to sit here and look out on my vast empty lawn. Nobody goes there now that the weather is cold—nobody from this place anyway—and the barren, absolutely flawless white blanket that covers it transfixes me. From somewhere under that diaphanous spread a light emanates that is strangely disseminated, as if Hyperion and Phoebus and Ra were all underneath dancing an intoxicated, frenzied jig. Even at night it radiates a phosphorescent afterglow that seems to kindle the lower boughs of the swaying pines. When I look out on my wasteland things begin to happen: puppet shows with remarkably human dolls dance across my private stage, life goes on little trips to yesterday. And sometimes my fantasies get away from me and scurry off toward the edge of time and I run after them in horror lest they leave me stranded here flopping in the dry dust of space where the imagination cannot breathe.

Two figures are standing on the lawn. One holds a brown rubber football tucked up under one arm and with his hand motions across the grass. The other, much smaller, runs in the direction that the finger points. They seem to be man and boy, perhaps father and son, but it is impossible to tell because they are faceless. Their features have been erased. Nylon stockings seem pulled down over their eyes and mouths. Two unfinished portraits passing a football across a lawn on a late summer afternoon. The air smells of salt and dry kelp and every so often there is a waft of lemon from the groves a half-mile inland. To their right, along a seawall, there is a row of twisted cypress that casts long shadows over the game, and as the boy runs for the ball that arcs through the afternoon, he moves through green patches of light and shadow.

Behind the figures there is a stand of eucalyptus that grows inland from the seawall. Pointed leaves hang downward like a thousand wind-chimes, and there is a constant rustle amidst the branches as if something alive is on the move. Beneath the grove, at its far corner, there is a low sprawling bungalow with several angular wings. A shake roof covered with bark gives it a thatched look, and its paint on the ocean side is weathered and peeling. There is a porch cantilevered over a thick growth of succulent that disappears under the house, and French doors open off the living room at the center of the deck. Four chairs made of aluminum pipe and plastic webbing lounge around a circular glass table, with a large sailcloth umbrella projecting from the middle.

The webbing on the chairs is a faded orange, and when the football arches over the cypress and crosses the wide golden path that leads across the water into tomorrow it turns orange in the reflection of the dying sun. It spirals along the seawall and descends back into the shadows toward the outstretched arms of the running boy, but it goes uncaught. Perhaps the light has played tricks with the boy's eyes. Perhaps the mask has obscured his vision. Who knows. Whatever the excuse, he trips and falls heavily just before the ball reaches him, and it bounds away over the wall onto the pebbled beach below. He scrambles to his feet and climbs down after it while the other figure at the far end of the lawn stands with hand on hip looking side ways through the cypress at the sea. There is a fiery track across the water and Santa Cruz island is visible on the horizon.

The scene repeats itself. The two faceless figures stand together while I take their picture. The hand motions and the boy runs through the mottled light. In the shadow of the cypress the arms stretch out for the floating ball and the light plays its trick once more. Or perhaps it is not the light. Perhaps it is something else. The ball is not overthrown, the boy is not running hard, the lawn is smooth and well mowed. The ball bounds over the seawall once again, and the boy picks himself up and scrambles after it.

When he returns his companion is gone and he hears the porch door of the bungalow slam. He stands for a time in the lengthening shadows tossing the ball into the air: catching and tossing, catching and tossing. Over and over. The motion becomes hypnotic. The boy is not real. He moves in slow motion. Catching and tossing, catching and tossing. He boots the ball high into the air and it twirls end over end in a slow, lazy flight above the cypress, a parabola of reflected light against the dark backdrop of the eucalyptus grove. And then the camera speeds up, the spell is broken, and he runs pell-mell in pursuit. In mock recovery of a goal-line fumble he dives on his ball.

He stands up and looks toward the bungalow. Motionless again he listens, as if he expects to hear his companion returning to the French doors on the porch. There is nothing, no sound but the gentle wash of the pebbles below the seawall and the wind-chimes in the eucalyptus. The sun is well below the horizon and the shadows have fled the approaching darkness. He watches an immense tidal wave of fog roll steadily in from the sea; a mighty, smoking bank of glaucous vapor that swallows everything in its path and that will soon engulf the house and silence the wind-chimes. The eucalyptus will turn into dripping, mist-shrouded giants, and will weep through the night on the roof of his room.

But the fog is paramorphic. When it rolls over the seawall it becomes solid and spreads a smooth, flawless blanket of snow across the lawn. The boy and the house dissolve, and there is only the fortress wall of ponderosa that terrifies the girl down the hall. I am left regarding my silent park and the lambent glow that flickers beneath its opaque surface, as if the fog that swallowed the sun could not quite digest its halo.

II

π This morning there is a boy with a machine eating paths in the covering on my lawn. He follows along behind his belching tool as it gobbles its way around the perimeter of the lawn, spewing snow out one side of its crooked jaws and farting a gaseous blue smoke that hangs motionless in the morning air. I run to complain that he is marring the finish on my landscape but they tell me we need to exercise. We can take walks now, even though it is winter. If the boy is not careful he will break through the thin crust that protects me from the eternal past.

When the machine finishes the outer edges of the lawn it begins very carefully to dissect its rectangle, moving slowly across the length of the park. When it reaches the far end it turns around and retraces its track exactly to the middle, where it stops and seems to ponder whether to angle to the left or the right. The smoke catches up to it and begins to disperse like a coastal mist evaporating in the first sun.

The boy raises the handle of his mower until it is perpendicular and rests his chin on the crossbar, looking across the lawn with its little piles and lumps of wet mown grass. A car pulls out from behind the white bungalow and moves down the drive. A man is driving and there is a woman next to him. Perhaps they are the boy's parents, but all faces are averted so that no resemblance among the three is apparent. The car stops for a moment and the woman, shading her eyes against the glare from the water, calls something to the boy. He nods and waves and continues his mowing, and the car moves down the drive until it is lost behind the plane trees that border the eastern edge of the property.

He mows carefully. Once he has carved his Maltese cross in the lawn he turns the mower over and pushes it down to a far corner and begins a diagonal line that intersects the other two in the middle. He has, when he is finished, a green Union Jack with dandelions. Leaving his machine, he runs up on the cantilevered porch to survey his art. Hip-shot, tennis shoes crossed, chin on hand, he leans on the rail for a bit, then goes and sprawls in an orange webbed chair under the deck umbrella.

The morning is bright and fresh. It is neither hot nor cool; just fresh. The succulent growing beneath the porch has tiny yellow flowers that attract the bees, and there is no sound but their drone and the intervaled swish of pebbles below the seawall. The ocean is calm and jeweled with tiny lights. The boy tilts back slightly in his chair, hands folded over the top of his crew cut, eyelids closed, face angled toward the sun. Behind a purple veil Hyperion and Phoebus and Ra dance a frenzied jig on an eyeball of china blue. The bees drone under the porch and time dies.

The sun has moved perceptibly when the boy stirs himself again and returns to his mowing. He cuts a circle in the middle of his flag, making an ornamental park of dandelion and crabgrass, and then, as if tired of his game, he shuts down his imagination and mows straight overlapping swatches back and forth across the lawn. He uses no catcher and the grass spews back on his legs, turning his tennis shoes a hairy green. He finishes all but a patch in front of the house and then, leaving the mower midway along one strip, he walks deliberately up the porch steps, brushes his jeans, and disappears.

Two pelicans flap sedately by, looking nearsighted as they peer into the swells beyond the seawall. The sun moves again along its course—suddenly—as if it had been drowsing and had forgotten what it was about: as if it had forgotten that down below a world of clocks grows impatient with its indolence. The porch door slams and the boy descends the steps, book in hand. He glances at the mower that has fallen asleep at its post, its long handle stretched out on the grass, and he crosses the lawn to the seawall. He climbs down onto the pebble beach, and putting his back against a boulder he begins to read.

> And the third angel sounded and there fell a great star from heaven, burning as it were a lamp, and it fell upon the third part of the rivers, and upon the fountains of waters;
>
> And the name of the star is called Wormwood: and the third part of the waters became wormwood; and many men died of the waters, because they were made bitter.

The boy is not aware that the car has returned his parents until he looks up startled at the human voice on the bank. The man's figure that belongs to the voice has a small round rock about the size of a fifty-cent piece in his palm and he shakes it as if he were about to cast a pair of dice. The boy lays his book down and gets to his haunches. He says something and starts to rise but the man flings the stone into the sea. It is not for sport. The gesture seems one of contempt or disgust, but it is hard to tell which. Perhaps it is both. When the boy climbs to the top of the seawall the lawn mower is lunching on the remaining grass. He goes and tries to take it, but the man gestures widely with his arm and flaps his hand toward the sea. His left sleeve is pinned at his waist and he pushes the mower with his belly while he motions away. The boy moves back a little and stands hunch-shouldered with his hands in his pockets watching the mower slice the uncut patch. When it is rolled away, upside down and clicking like a geared bicycle, he wanders along behind it into the garage.

The man has disappeared and the boy stands at the edge of the driveway flipping pebbles into the foliage. He walks slowly out toward the plane trees and follows the drive to where it dips steeply and crosses the railroad track at the end of the property. He leaves the road and climbs the bank above the track and walks down along it through sour grass and nasturtium and ice plant. The ground cover is spongy and wet under his feet and his tennis shoes are soon soaked. The air is pungent with eucalyptus and earth mold and the fragrance of lemon from the nearby groves.

Down the tracks two boys, both about his size, are balancing their way along the rails, their hands full of little hard seed pods that they throw at each other as they go. From the bank he watches them work their way until they are abreast of him and then past. The larger of the two he recognizes from his school and he half raises a hand in greeting, but there is no signal returned and neither of the boys speaks. When they are ten or fifteen yards past, the smaller of the two spins around on the track and fires a pod at him with implausible accuracy. It stings him on the neck just above his shirt collar and he quickly fishes in the ice plant until he finds a rock which he hurls back. He misses, hitting the rail instead, and it sings with metallic vibration up and down the line. The boys scamper to the side of the roadbed and begin throwing large chunks of cinder and gravel at him and he ducks behind a tree, digging stones out from around its roots and firing them as fast as he can. The barrage of stone and cinder continues for ten minutes without a score, but then, as he finds a flinty rock almost the size of his fist and flings it blindly down the bank at his attackers, he hears a howl of shocked pain and peers from behind his cover to see his initial assailant down on the track ties, holding his left temple with both hands as a crimson rivulet begins to course down his cheek and fan out along his jaw. The howl continues at an unaltered pitch as the larger boy, gesturing and shouting threats at the bank, helps his companion back down the track in the direction from which they came.

The boy squats in the ice plant for a time, smelling the earth mold and lemon. It is very still, and hot. A bluebottle fly hums in toward him, the volume of its drone increasing, louder and louder, and then suddenly diminishing as it veers sharply off into the vegetation. Finally he stands, and begins to walk back toward the house. As he nears the garage he can hear the telephone ringing and he pauses. The ringing stops and he waits. Four minutes. Five. He hears his name called from the porch and he walks slowly down to the lawn and across to the steps. He does not go up, but stands on the grass and looks away at the cypress as the voices speak to him from the deck. A woman is talking, his mother perhaps, but she seems to be addressing the eucalyptus grove at the other end of the porch. And then a man, sitting in one of the webbed chairs that is angled so that he is really confronting the French doors of the house. There is no unity in this picture, no focus. The boy shakes his head at the cypress. No. Not me. He points to the seawall and to the book lying on a flat rock under a tree, shakes his head again, shrugs, denies. The voices fade and there is only the droning of the bees in the succulent and the wash of pebbles on the narrow shore.

He goes partway up the steps and turns around, arms still on the railings. Hoisting himself into the air he comes back down on the next step. He makes a paralytic, backward ascent to the top and stands there looking over the lawn at the still-faint image of the paths he mowed that morning. There is the impress of a rectangle cut into four squares with a diagonal line running across it. Where the lines intersect in the middle there is a circle ten feet in diameter.

The air is very bright and fresh. It sparkles like a ground-glass screen as tiny particles of frozen moisture float down from the gently swaying pines. The blue fog has vanished, the boy and his snow machine are gone. But my landscape has undergone another transmutation, and I look down at a Tuileries garden without vegetation; an ornamental layout of unreality.

As I look it begins to snow, soft, heavy flakes at first, drifting feathers from a pillow I once tossed into a ceiling fan in a hotel room in Los Angeles. How ironic that the boy should have worked all morning clearing paths that will now fill up again, silently, until all is as level and unmarred as before he began. How shallow the inroads. How useless the attempts. Even if time had not erased every visible trace of his labor nobody would have walked out there anyway. We stay behind our walls here. Nobody wants to go outside to be reminded of his mortality. We look on eternal nature and it becomes a metaphor for time.

The lawn is even again, blank, empty. It is a page without print, a canvas without pictures. It is I who must fill it in. Nature has no imagination: art is not its business.

> *And there was given me a reed like unto a rod: and the angel stood, saying, Rise, and measure the temple of God, and the altar, and them that worship therein.*

My figures are back on the altar. The man and the boy and the ball. They stand on the lawn; one points and the other runs. The man is still faceless but I see in the boy's china blue eyes the reflection of myself, running, arms outstretched for the orange ball that floats down out of a dying sky. And I see the boy fall before it happens. His eyes are a mirror of his mind and they picture yet another boy running: running through the mottled shade of cypress, along paths that intersect and return upon each other, until finally he stumbles out of the maze and onto a fiery track of sunlight on water that leads out over an endless horizon. There is a tinkle of wind-chimes in the air. And the boy is running with arms outstretched. Running to fall down.

III

π Tonight is completely empty. In the corridor I turn off the overhead lights so that I can look out the big picture window at the end without seeing myself staring back in. No moon tonight, no stars; only relief. The mountain slopes away from this side of the building, down through miles of pine forest and meadows to the Feather River where it begins to sputter into rolling grassland and finally collapses into a broad flat plain. During the day the mountain is quiet. Now and then a chain saw snarls off in some invisible canyon, but otherwise it is silent, resting, waiting for darkness. At night, when the winds begin to sweep over its crest and down through the draws that corrugate its side, it howls a continuous song of isolation. Perched up here on its southern flank we are sorry companions to its solitude.

As I peer out the window into this black void, a tiny light weaves along in aimless confusion; disappearing, reappearing, turning back upon itself, jogging left and then right, disappearing again. Watching it I feel as if I am standing in front of an immense black oscilloscope in a dark and empty room, plotting the course of a dream along the spaceless eternity of my mind.

Years ago, on just such a night as this, the headlights of a nightmare coasted down through the blackness of pine woods and blasted granite and out into a dreary landscape of red rock and sand and hatred and despair. Behind the headlights sit a man and a boy: the same boy, the same mower of paths that I knew at another time and in another place. He is older now, taller. There is a faint shadow on his upper lip and two blemishes on his forehead, but his eyes are the same color of blue china. The man is different. He is thin and balding and wears steel-rimmed glasses and there is a kind of nervous energy in all his motions, even as he guides the coasting car down the mountain.

They drift in silence. I notice that the clock glowing faintly green next to the glove compartment has broken, its malformed arms stretched at a quarter to three. Crucified. Or perhaps it's not broken. Perhaps it just quit. Gave up. After it chased itself around and around twenty million times it began to perceive its own absurdity and one afternoon at a quarter to three said to the faded face of a plaid seat cushion, "Screw it, I quit," and settled back to take a rest. Its tongue hangs out of a fast-slow grin and it watches the occupants of the car with obvious indifference. The wiry man behind the wheel is apparently uncomfortable with the boy. He seems to want to make conversation and frequently glances over at his charge, but he says nothing. He has a nervous tic in the muscle by his right eye. The boy, on the other hand, obviously does not want to talk and he stares sullenly out the side window at the darkness rushing past. Although the two have been acquainted for less than an hour (a fact to which the clock is impervious) there seems already a considerable tension between them.

In the back seat the boy's trunk joggles and sways on the cushions. In it, I seem to remember, there is a charcoal gray suit, a sport coat, a half dozen neckties, and a collection of Levi's and work shirts. There is also a neat pile of school supplies in one corner: a fountain pen and matching pencil, a ruler, notepaper, a dictionary, and a package of addressed and stamped envelopes. Under a pile of T-shirts and underwear he has concealed a carton of cigarettes, though he has been told that smoking is against the rules except for upper classmen at a specified time and place.

The lights pick up an approaching fork in the road and the car slows and swings to the left onto an unpaved track that winds across a low rolling desert of sagebrush and cactus. To the east the night is beginning to pale and the sky looks like an inverted black bowl on which the glaze failed to take along part of the rim. Fantastic shapes begin to emerge as the car rolls out of the darkness: colonnades of smooth rock that stand like chessmen on a surrealistic board of sage and sand; spires and monuments that would dwarf the imagination of a Pharaoh. Out of the night a holy land slowly appears: cathedrals of towering red rock that glow like burnished gold as the dawn strikes their buttressed walls.

But in this waking dream the boy is falling asleep and is unaware that he is no longer in the pine forest on the mountain. When the car stops in a compound of low cinder-block buildings, he has a vision of a man carrying his trunk down a narrow hall, and when the vision turns to reality he finds himself in an eight-by-ten cubicle in which, a dim and mysterious voice seems to tell him, he is to pass the rest of his life.

The days drag in this holy land. From the window of his room he confronts, every morning and night, a gigantic monument to his isolation that rises less than a mile away out of the sage and red dust: an incredible temple that turns red and black in an endless cycle of dawns and dusks: a massive reflection of the alternating rage and despair that consume his waking hours. There is only the relief of night and sleep from the glaring redness of the land. Its grit makes every breath abrasive. It filters into the buildings and turns clothes and books and sheets a pale pink that won't wash out because even the water contains its dye. Its film is always in the eyes. Red dust in the nose. Taste of redness in my mouth.

The high priest of the monastery is the nervous, balding man with steel-rimmed eyes, and he is like the omnipresent dust, filtering his own tensions and fears and agitations into every life in his charge. He is obsessed with rules, regulations, directions. On the corners of the buildings there are signs to assist the confused. There are books and pamphlets and lists on proper conduct. No smoking, no swearing, no spitting. No talking, no laughing, no singing. Check the listings posted in the dining hall for weekly assigned friends. Dancing *is* permitted. On Friday and Saturday morning after breakfast and before lunch. Dancers will maintain a minimum distance of eight inches. Mixed-couple outings are forbidden. Mixed swimming is forbidden. Kissing is forbidden. Masturbation and insanity are forbidden. Section eight of our penal code expressly forbids everything not herein forbidden.

A council for disciplinary action meets every week to judge and punish (the two are inseparable). The members sit in a darkened room with hoods over their faces so that the accused will not recognize possible participators in his offense. The boy is not a member of the council but he meets with it regularly.

"Ryan, you are accused of smoking in the laundry room on Thursday night after lights-out. How do you plead?"

"Where are the others?"

"What others?"

"There were at least seven other guys there. How come I'm the only one that's caught?"

"Then you admit your guilt?"

"Sure, but . . ."

"You are confined to your room for two days and permitted to communicate with no one."

The council files solemnly out the back door leaving the criminal standing on a low wooden platform. He and I recognize two of his partners in the laundry by the boots that stick out from beneath their robes.

The council meets again and again, and always the boy meets with it. "Ryan, we have a letter here that informs us that you have ignored the assignment-of-friends rule, and that last week, when your assigned friend came to go with you to compulsory conversation hour at Miss Dikes', you told him, and I paraphrase from his letter, to have intercourse with himself. How do you plead?"

"What difference does it make?"

"Since you are not interested in making friends here, we have asked that a card table be placed in the center of the dining hall, and that you take your meals from now on by yourself."

"Same time as everybody else?"

"Of course."

There is a path worn in the sand leading out through sage and greasewood toward the red rock cathedral that lies to the east of the afternoon, and Ryan, with a shadow on his lip and a book in his hand, shuffles along it like a weary fugitive, his squaw boots detonating little explosions of red dust that float backward and dissolve in his wake. Behind him a single cumulous cloud sneaks up behind a mesa and rests its black potbelly on the rim, waiting for the reinforcements marching along behind the San Francisco Mountains.

The boy leaves the main route toward the rocks and follows a lesser trail that angles northeast along the bottom of a rocky wash. After a quarter mile he climbs out and cuts down across a sloping field of cactus and piñon towards a long snaky line of willow and cottonwood that marks the path of a creek flowing out of a distant canyon and across the lower plains.

He makes his way through the willows to a sandy open clearing along the bank of the stream, and flopping himself down next to a fallen cottonwood limb he opens the book and begins to read. Is it poetry? Yes. I remember. Yeats. I remember it all because of the prophetic poem. He lay in the sand and read it aloud:

> "I went out to the hazel wood,
> Because a fire was in my head,
> And cut and peeled a hazel wand,
> And hooked a berry to a thread—"

There is a tune to this, he said. It's a song, not a poem, or else it's both. A counselor at camp used to sing it. Many times. He was a great guitar player and this is one of the songs he used to sing to us at night.

> "And when white moths were on the wing,
> And moth-like stars were flickering out,
> I dropped the berry in a stream
> And caught a little silver trout."

Behind him the willows rustled and a girl from the school appeared at the edge of the clearing. Pretty hair and startled eyes, but homely. "Hello," he said. "I'm just reading about you."

She came across the sand to the cottonwood limb. "Reading about me?"

"Yes. This poem." He showed her the book. "It's about a man who goes fishing in the willows like here, and he catches a trout and it turns into a beautiful woman." He read her the first stanza.

She gave a wry smile. "You're not reading about me."

"Listen," he said. "Listen to the rest of this.

> "When I had laid it on the floor
> I went to blow the fire a-flame,
> But something rustled on the floor,
> And someone called me by my name:
> It had become a glimmering girl
> With apple blossom in her hair
> Who called me by my name and ran
> And faded through the brightening air."

"What a funny boy you are," she said. "At school you're

always in trouble, and then you come down here and read poetry to yourself."

The willows rustled again along the far side of the clearing. "Did anyone come here with you?" he asked.

"No. I always come alone. Maybe that's your glimmering girl." She laughed.

"You come here often?"

"Sometimes."

The willows crackled again, but in a different place, and the boy rose to his knees and looked over the log.

"It must be an animal," the girl said. "Read the rest of the poem."

He sat down again with his back against the limb and found his place.

> "Though I am old with wandering
> Through hollow lands and hilly lands,
> I will find out where she has gone,
> And kiss her lips and take her hands;
> And walk among long dappled grass,
> And pluck till time and times are done
> The silver apples of the moon,
> The golden apples of the sun."

She was sitting in the sand beside him now, and when he finished reading he looked at her homely face. Her lashes were very long and her eyes were closed. "I like that poem," she said. "The golden apples of the sun." He leaned over and kissed her on the mouth for a long time. She didn't respond, but she didn't pull away either, and when he moved back she said, "I'm no silver trout and there certainly are no apple blossoms in this godforsaken place."

A wind had come up and the poplars were shivering before the approaching storm. A clap of thunder pealed in the distance and bounced back at itself off the rims of the surrounding mesas. They rose and he led her out through the willows just as heavy silver drops began to patter around them in the thick red dust.

The council files solemnly back into the room and the lights dim. Behind the hollow ringing of their boots a muffled drum rolls, and the criminal, seated in a wooden chair, watches intently as two hooded figures roll back a prop screen to reveal an auburn-haired green-eyed girl seated high on a plaster throne covered with seaweed and poppies. But there is something wrong in the picture. When she smiles her teeth are black as if she had a negative mouth in a positive face. The drum roll subsides and she rises to her feet.

"You are accused of the murder of . . ." She pauses in mid-sentence and peers at her victim. ". . . But you are so young, and how is it that he had blond hair and yours is dark?"

A voice from behind the plaster throne shouts, "Cut . . . cut. You're reading the wrong place in the script, Martha. Let's try it again from the beginning."

The drum starts its roll and the green eyes stare down again from their perch. "Ryan. You have been discovered in the willow grove by the creek, kissing the girl named Lola Wright, and the council regards your offense this week too great for it to handle. We have summoned the faculty board which now awaits your appearance." And the throne and girl and hooded figures fade out and the drum rolls in a new setting.

In the living room of the high priest's house the faculty board sits in grave silence. The curtains are pulled and when Ryan opens his eyes the sun is switched on behind their blue folds to give the room a smoky appearance.

The members sit in the murky light with stocking masks pulled over their faces. From a far corner of the room a plaintive voice wails *"Unclean . . . unclean."* Over and over in a background chant to the deeper, calmer voice that begins the accusation. "Ryan. Your conduct in the willow grove on Wednesday afternoon is unspeakable. If you had not been rooting around with that disgusting waitress while your boy followed his ball off the cliff and . . ."

A voice in the background cuts in. "Hold it. Hold it. Jesus Christ, can't any of you people get your lines right? Come on, Al, dammit. Let's try it once more."

"Ryan. Your conduct in the willow grove on Wednesday afternoon is unspeakable. Lola Wright's counselor, Miss Dikes, was so revolted that she went immediately and drew herself a hot bath."

"Unclean . . . unclean . . . unclean . . . unclean."

"She insisted, of course, that Miss Wright do the same. We think of no satisfactory way to deal with you and we are unable to dwell on this disgusting problem."

"Unclean . . . unclean."

"Our inadequate sentence is that you shall be placed on probation for the remainder of the year, and that you shall stand in the shower in your dormitory for the rest of this day."

"Unclean . . . unclean."

"Hopefully some of the filth will be washed from your hide."

"Unclean."
"But all I did was kiss her."
"Unclean . . . unclean . . . unclean."

The boy walks back to his room. Another storm is moving down from the mountains to the north and lightning flashes in the San Francisco peaks. As he passes upwind of the director's car, parked at the edge of the compound, he scuffs his feet through the dust and raises a large red cloud that blows like a pink mist down on the cream-colored sedan. The car has just been washed and the gesture is not wholly futile. "Unclean, unclean."

He goes into the dormitory, ignoring the shower stalls that stand waiting, and walks to his room. Leaving the door open he fishes around in a dresser drawer and comes up with a pack of Lucky Strikes. He picks one out and lights it, throwing the pack on the desk, and then sits on the edge of his bunk facing the window. Beyond a sea of juniper and sage the fiery walls and polished spires of his temple flicker briefly in a darkening sky, until, with a distant roll of thunder, their radiance is suddenly eclipsed.

IV

π And I am back in my dark hall, straining into the void for another glimpse of the pinprick light that has been meandering through my dream, coming closer and closer as I stand with my face pressed against the glass. Suddenly it reappears far below me, tangled in a thicket of pines. It hangs motionless . . . winks out . . . on again . . . bursts free from the waving arms that grasp at it . . . and splits in two. Like identical meteors in a topsy-turvy world the lights climb straight up out of the black canyon and just when I think they will slam into the walls beneath me, they burn out, leaving me groping in a rust-colored haze. My eyes are infrared bulbs weakly illuminating a darkroom full of developing pictures. Taste of red in my mouth. Dusty air that rakes like sandpaper in my nostrils. The images grow clearer in the vaporous solution that fills the corridor. I sweat in the heat of a desert afternoon, smelling mesquite and piñon, and watch the boy as he walks across a flagstone patio and knocks on the kitchen door of a large adobe house.

A chestnut-haired woman answers the door. Wrinkles around the eyes and mouth, tanned face, hazel eyes, and a smile. She beckons him in and he follows her into a small sunny room off the kitchen where her sewing lies across the arm of a stuffed chair. "You need a haircut," she says, and runs her cool fingers through the mane that covers his neck and creeps over his shirt collar. "When Matt is through bending your cars, I'll lower them for you." When she smiles the sides of her face crinkle all around her eyes.

I watch him walk through the house, following the noise of a typewriter to a spacious, book-lined studio. At the door he clears his throat and the gray-haired man at the desk turns around with a hello and waves him in. "Lemme finish this sentence," he says, and the boy sits down in a bowl-shaped cowhide chair.

The room has a high beamed ceiling and a large mustard and gray Navajo rug on the floor, and the desk at which Matt Stevenson types is massive and carved in Spanish designs. The chairs are all hide-bottomed and many of the books are bound in leather. On the wall a Cantu etching of the Madonna and her baby smile down and make the boy feel strangely comfortable.

When the man finally turns from the typewriter and speaks, his tone is as mild and pleasant as the Madonna's eyes, and the boy is for a time unaware of a voice in the room.

". . . to have you stop by. Would you like a cigarette?"

"I'm not allowed, sir."

"Yes, I know. But in my house I make my own rules."

He rubs his hands through his grizzled crew cut and

stretches his long legs out in front of the desk. The boy does not smoke and Stevenson does not repeat his offer.

"Have you heard from your father recently, Ryan?" he asks.

"Couple weeks ago, I guess."

"Your mother is still living in the Santa Barbara place?"

"Yes. It hasn't been sold yet."

Stevenson leans over the desk and takes a cigarette from the open box on the blotter. He lights it and sprawls in his chair, hands across his stomach. "I'm not trying to pry, so don't answer this if you don't want to. But how do you feel about the divorce?"

"I don't know." The boy shrugs. "I guess it's their business."

"But you resent being packed off to school while it goes on."

"No. . . . I don't know. . . ." Another shrug. "I don't think so."

Stevenson takes a drag on his cigarette. "You know, I guess, that your father and I went to college together and that we were in the same company during the war."

"Yes, sir. He's told me."

"I was part of the jeep accident that cost him his arm. He became quite a different person after that. Impatient. Anyone offered to help him he'd bite their heads off. I think he became a little hard to live with."

"My mother thinks so."

Stevenson snuffs the butt out in the ashtray and gets out of his chair. He walks to the window. "My being here at this school has a lot to do with your being sent here. Your father thought that a change of scene would be good for you, and a friend in camp would make it easier. Unfortunately my heart chose a poor time to start acting up."

"I wrote my father that you'd been in the hospital most of the year."

"Well, I think I'm back in shape," Stevenson replies. "And maybe we can do something now to straighten out the problems you seem to have created. I gather you've been in trouble since you got here."

"Yes, sir."

"Well it happens to the best of us. I've asked Warden to tell the council that from now on if you get into hot water you're to be sent to me. But you don't need to wait for that. The door is open anytime. You want some ice tea?"

And I see the boy leaving the adobe house just as the sun dips below a distant mesa. He crosses the flagstone patio and goes lightly down the steps. His hair has been cut and the look on his face is less sullen. As he walks down the path toward the dormitory he is whistling and then he breaks into part of a song.

> "I went out to the hazel wood,
> Because a fire was in my head,
> And cut and peeled a hazel wand,
> And hooked a berry to a thread . . ."

Stevenson's study keeps coming back. The leather books, the Navajo rug; faint smell of cowhide and oiled wood. In the ice tea there is always fruit juice; fragrance of lemon and clove. Stevenson is telling the boy about Mexican painters, showing prints and original drawings. The Cantu Madonna smiles from the wall. The mustard and gray of the rug blend into the soft sand tones of a desert scene drawn by some Indian artist: a fawn-colored antelope stands on a slight rise, smelling the wind that carries a strange scent out of a buff and red wash. An unseen hunter kicks loose a stone from its rocky bank and the antelope vanishes in a cloud of sand and wind that blows south and onto the rug.

The study is a sanctuary, a shrine, presided over by Stevenson and the Madonna. When the sun scorches the flagstone patio outside and sends shimmering waves up past the windows, the thick adobe walls keep the inside cool. When a storm blows in from the San Francisco Mountains and the desert shivers in a wet, cold wind, a warm fire burns in the beehive-shaped fireplace in one corner of the room. The tea is hot then, and a lemon-clove steam rises out of the cups.

The boy sits in a straight chair next to the fire, his shirt off, and he hugs his arms to his sides while cool hands guide a pair of shears through the hair that grows over his collar. "I'm sorry Matt isn't here today," the woman says. "But emergencies come up, even out here. He's been so pleased with the way you've been going along lately, he was going to give you one of the Cantu prints you liked. For your room. Don't tell him I mentioned it. It's his surprise."

The shears work up around one ear and the trimming is done. She brushes him off with a towel and he puts his shirt back on, working his shoulder blades around to scratch the itches. "Let me get rid of this hair and we'll have some tea." And she is gone.

The boy wanders around the study. At a low corner cabinet near the fireplace he pauses . . . listens . . . bends over and opens it. Bottles arranged neatly on the two shelves. Glasses in racks on the doors. Scotch, bourbon, numerous liqueurs, Rose's Lime Juice, bitters. He closes the cabinet and walks to an open rack across the room where Stevenson keeps his Mexican prints and drawings, flips through, pulls one or two out, replaces them, returns to the liquor cabinet. He stands again in front of it, hands in his back pockets, and pulls the doors open with his tennis shoe. Then he stoops, and for no reason whatever, except that he should not, should not, should not, he removes a pint of Old Forester and a can of smoked oysters, and slips them into the pocket of his jacket lying on the desk.

"Come in the kitchen, Ryan. Let's have tea in here."

May Day, visitors' day, all the students laugh and play. The decree comes down from the high priest. Prospective pupils and their parents are coming. All rooms will be cleaned and scrubbed. Inmates will be industriously employed at their desks. Faculty members will be leading groups through the dorms all afternoon. Be washed and dressed. Wear a necktie.

This is the day to escape. This is the day to break free. Ryan moves methodically through his room. I see him sweeping piles of soiled laundry into the closet. Books, shoes, dirty shirts, old socks. Slam the door, open it, rearrange and try again. A mountain of papers on the desk, a stale box of broken cookies, a Coke-stained folder of charcoal drawings. Lug them out back to the incinerator. Borrow the broom from the boys down the hall and sweep out the red sand. Taste of red on the tongue. Windpipe like garnet paper. Here comes the inspector. Here comes Warden to tell you to start all over.

The door swings open. A twitching muscle behind steel-rimmed glasses, bulging forehead that glistens like wet marble. "Place looks like Coney Island, Mister. Get a mop and start scrubbing the crud off this floor." The door slams and Ryan raises his middle finger at it.

Borrow the mop from the boys down the hall. Wring it out in the sink and watch the water run red. Back to the room and swab the deck. The closet pops open. Boots, laundry, a pile of *National Geographics* spill out onto the damp floor and get crammed back in.

"Mail call, mail call. Here's a couple for you, Ryan."

A couple for you, Ryan. Letters from home. He stretches out on the bed and closes his eyes. Outside his closed door boys are running back and forth with pails and mops and brooms, shouting at each other, cursing. "Come on, ya sonofabitch. Hurry up with that. Warden's given me five to square away." A pail clangs to the floor in a room down the hall, followed by an angry shriek. "Now look, ya simple asshole. Ya soaked my sack."

He sits up and swings his legs off the bed, bends over between them, and pulls a footlocker from underneath. He snaps the clamps and raises the lid, then gets up and fastens the bolt on the door. From the bottom of the locker he takes a pint of Old Forester and a can of smoked oysters and returns with them to his bunk.

One eye opens and stares dully at the molding where the floor and the wall join. Where the angle should be there is only a flat plane: white wall, gray molding, brown floor. The cracks between the boards keep shifting their direction, pointing right and then left like a series of compass needles following a magnet. For the space of two or three feet out in front of the eye the boards are submerged beneath a puddle, and beyond the puddle in the cracks little creeks are pioneering their way toward the molding. The glassy surface is broken here and there by what appear to be black rocks; little sea stacks that smell like seaweed or kelp or, perhaps, oysters. The waters are calm for a bit, until suddenly from midpoint in the body that lies stretched on the floor behind the puddle there is a tremendous convulsion and a mouth, down somewhere beneath the eye, opens and a fresh wave washes across the surface. The sea stacks are rearranged and new ones crop up near a chin and a nose. The eyelid slides closed, as if in relief, and the waters become calm once more.

When the eye opens again it is responding to a call from the ear. Outside the room voices are carrying on, laughing, talking, and feet are approaching the door. The ear seems to recognize a mild, pleasant tone but it is not certain. The door opens and the voices, quite suddenly, stop. The head shifts painfully and the eye encounters an anguished response in the gaze of Matt Stevenson, leaning against the doorjamb with one hand half covering his face.

The trunk is repacked. The charcoal gray suit, a sport coat, two neckties (the other four have been lost), a depleted collection of Levi's and work shirts. The fountain pen and matching pencil are also missing, but there is the package of addressed and stamped envelopes in the same corner in which it arrived. It gives no evidence of having diminished.

A pickup truck with a pipe railing four feet above the perimeter of its bed swings into the compound and stops before the cinder-block dormitory. Its muffler has blown and it idles like a motorboat. The steel-rimmed glasses come out of the dorm carrying the trunk and throw it unceremoniously into the back. The boy, an empty sack of vomit-soiled skin, is flung in behind it, and the truck roars out past the buildings and onto the dusty red track that wanders toward the mountains through cactus and juniper. It jolts back onto the paved highway, and after an hour begins to climb the winding switchback road into the sun.

And as the truck breaks out of the timber at the top and rolls along through a lush meadow sprinkled with buttercup and lupine, the boy stands and grips the crossbar above the cab and begins to sing.

> "Though I am old with wandering
> Through hollow lands and hilly lands . . ."

With his face into the wind and his knuckles white on the bar he sings loud above the roar of the broken muffler beneath him, so loud that the workman driving him out of his nightmare turns around inside the cab and glances up through the rear window.

> "And walk among long dappled grass
> And pluck till time and times are done,
> The silver apples of the moon,
> The golden apples of the sun."

PART Two

I

π Spring, and the last of the snow is gone. The grass that has been hibernating all winter is beginning to stretch and turn green again. There are two Japanese gardeners cultivating the beds around the edge of the lawn, scraping their three-pronged diggers around in the moist black earth, and the grounds keeper tromps around in his rubber boots inspecting, pointing, clipping, pulling, calling directions to his helpers.

My mother had a Japanese gardener after my father left Santa Barbara; a funny little man, wizened and gray-skinned, who picked the snails off the shrubs and ate them, and who turned everything he cast his eye upon into a bouquet. One afternoon in the early fall he didn't come to work because he died, but it didn't matter. The place had been sold. My mother was moving farther north where there were no unpleasant "associations." Pulling up roots is no problem. They never go deep in California.

But associations. They are hard to escape. You run and run and run but they follow right along. Japanese gardeners, trails of slime on the dew-wet grass, a crunching snack at the end of the rainbow. He ate the small ones shells and all. Collect a handful and sit on the seawall under a cypress and pop them juicy into your mouth as you look out over the kelp-cluttered ocean.

Long pointed leaves rustle in the dry afternoon. Pods shaped like coolie hats, their summer fringe of red now withered and brown, drop on the thatched roof of the sprawling bungalow beneath the eucalyptus grove. On the ocean side of the house the yellow paint is faded and peeling, showing the old white underneath, and the redwood deck that cantilevers over the succulent bed is splotched with gull droppings. An inland breeze blows sporadically across the water, making black fans on an otherwise flat and leaden sea. In the driveway behind the house two burly cigar smokers with sweat moons on their tan shirts are closing the doors of a Mayflower van while a woman in a bright-colored print dress gives them directions.

". . . One-o-four Seabright Lane . . . Santa Cruz . . . the front door should be open." Perfecto Perfecto nods and Panatella drops ashes on a book in which his pen is noting the address. "Just put everything in the proper rooms and I'll have it moved around later."

As the van rolls out the drive the woman goes through the garage and back into the house. High heels on oak floors echo in the hollow rooms. From a doorway at one end of the kitchen she calls down a dark hall toward the rear of the house. "Going into town for a few minutes, Ryan. Close up some last minute things. Finish your packing, please, before I get back." There is no reply and she waits a moment.

"Are you in there?"

"Yeah."

"Are you packing?"

"Yeah."

"Why didn't you answer me?"

"Didn't know an answer was required."

She is irritated by his insolence and starts an angry reply but stops, realizes that this is the response he hopes for. "Just be ready when I get back, please. 'Bout a half hour. I want to be well up the coast before dark."

He sits at his desk under the window. There is a picture of a man in uniform on the wall and a suitcase on the floor. There is a long box on the desk. Otherwise the room is an empty shell. No furniture, no rug, no lamps, no curtain. The boy takes something apart. I see that it is a model ship about three feet long, unfinished, though its masts are stepped and various blocks are glued on the hull that re semble . . . will resemble . . . cabins and hatches. And from somewhere out of the past I seem to hear a voice, hollow and flat. Perhaps it comes from the uniformed man on the wall.

"Ryan, the answer once and for all is no. I am not going to give you, or even loan you, thirty bucks for a model ship."

"I'll pay you back, Dad."

"Yes? Out of what?"

"Out of my paper-route money."

"That paper route that your mother and I are always taking for you? Seems to me that you owe me most of that magnificent bankroll already. . . . Well . . . don't you? And don't get that petulant, bawl-baby look on your face."

"I'm not going to bawl, and I will pay you back."

"The money is not the point. I know exactly what will happen to that model if you get it. You'll spend about three days wondering why you can't put it together and then it will sit in your closet along with a thousand other failures like the guitar you never learned to play and the airplane you never got to fly and the chemistry set you never used. Forget it. The answer is no."

Spars have been installed on the foremast and the mizzenmast, and the rudder and bowsprit glued in the proper places. The fife rails have been set into the deck three-quarters of an inch and the keel sanded smooth and fastened along the bottom of the hull. In little packages on the desk there are tiny metal belaying pins and pulleys for the rigging, anchors, and capstans, a wheel, chains, and barrels. Again I hear the voice.

"Ryan, where did you get the money for that model?"

"From my paper route."

"You're lying. You make less than fifteen dollars a month on that route. Come on, bub, where did you get it?"

"I borrowed the rest from a kid at school."

"Jesus! You can't even lie worth a damn. You can just forget about going up to scout camp this summer. I'll think of some chores for you to do around here to work off what you stole."

The desk is littered with parts that are still to go on. Progress seems to have stopped when the spars were installed. But I am confused. Take two steps back. He is dismantling progress and packing it carefully in a long narrow box. On top he folds a colored picture of the ship from which his is modeled, an 880-ton bark heeling over in a strong gale, and then he shuts the lid.

On the floor his suitcase is closed and the room is empty

except for a few crumpled papers in the corner and the desk that is built in under the window. The wooden floors creak and pop throughout the house as if old ghosts of the departing past have suddenly absolved them of some heavy secret. Or perhaps it's just the shifting foundation. The eucalyptus leaves rustle. Faint sound of wind-chimes. Hands in his pockets, he stands a few moments listening to the pods drop on the roof, then picks up the box and the suitcase and the sixteen years and walks out of the empty house. He leaves the uniformed man hanging on the dark wall.

II

π I went outside for the first time today and lay on the lawn beneath my window. It seemed rather strange after months of looking out at this pine-guarded park to be suddenly down in it looking back up. The sky was very blue and feathery little clouds kept wandering down from the high mountains and disappearing over the rim of the building. The sun was hot on the grass and when I closed my eyes I could almost imagine myself on the beach below our new house in Santa Cruz.

Santa Cruz. A beachhead out of time. An interlude of surf and sand, fog and sun. Happy scenes in endless succession. Sing, "All the good times are past and gone." I had a buddy called Milton the Mole. Myopic Milty. Wonderful surfer, straight A in mathematics, terrible driver. Six years, six accidents. One fatality. Just one. When he stepped back into time.

The head gardener is lecturing again, over across the lawn. He gestures with his trowel, takes a long pointed stick and draws an isosceles triangle in the soft earth and hands a flat of seedlings to one of his helpers. Formal gardens. Geometric designs. We live in the eighteenth century.

In front of a blackboard with a "Santa Cruz Unified School District" label the head gardener lectures on mysterious theorems. He gestures with his pointed stick and draws an isosceles triangle on the slate with a piece of colored chalk. I see that he has only one arm and that he wears steel-rimmed glasses. Apparently it is not an isosceles triangle that he draws but an imitation of an Indian sand painting. "You will notice," he says, "that the texture of time in both Mexican and Indian art is often created by mixing large quantities of sunlight into the pigment of space."

In the second aisle at the back of the room the boy sits and dreams of hot sand baking in the sun and the pound of surf in the cove near his house. Intervaled swish of water running back over the pebbles. WHOMP. A wave smashes down on the backwash of its predecessor and spreads out over the beach, starts its own backwash and then, after a moment of absolute silence, WHOMP—a new mountain crests and rolls its foam into the mouth of the cove.

He realizes suddenly that papers have been passed out and the class is taking a quiz. He looks at the question and begins to work the problem, but after a few minutes he knows he can't do it and he gives up. Around him heads are bent over desks, pencils scratching in blue exam books, furious erasing, more scratching, more erasing. He looks across the aisle at a cheerful looking blond boy whose glasses are perched midway down on his peanut-shell nose. Milton Lewis. Straight A student. Sloppy goof who looks uncoordinated but who has a local reputation as a fine surfer. Also said to be completely inept with the women. He is known around as Mole.

Mole glances over at the boy, squints, winks, and goes back to his exam. Ryan tries to return to the beach but the daydream has gone. He doodles on his paper and thinks dully about the senior counselor's warning that if he fails geometry he will not likely get into college. "So what," he says to himself.

Ryan feels a piece of paper being slipped onto his desk and he looks up. Mole winks at him again and goes back to checking his answer. On the paper Ryan sees the question worked out in a hasty but clear hand and he quickly copies it. When the bell rings he hands it in with the rest of the class.

During the lunch break Ryan finds his prompter eating a Swiss cheese sandwich at the top of the bleachers by the baseball diamond. As he climbs up, Mole waves and grins his foolish grin. "Didja get it in?" he calls.

"Yes. Listen . . . thanks very much."

"S'okay."

"I'd have been screwed without help."

Mole munches on his Swiss cheese and then offers Ryan one of the two apples he has in his sack. "Didn't look like you knew the answers. How you doing in there?"

"In geometry? I'm busting it."

They sit on the hard wooden bench and eat the apples. At the foot of the bleachers towhees are scratching in the dirt for lunch crumbs. Ryan fires his core into the bushes alongside third base and the birds flit away.

"Where you going to college?" Mole asks.

"If I flunk geometry, I'm not."

"That close, huh?"

"So says Mr. Bricker."

Mole searches the bottom of his lunch sack and comes up with a Hershey bar. "Want some?" he asks.

"No. Thanks."

"Ah   listen. . . . If you want I can help you out with the math."

"Keep passing me the answers?"

"Naw. We'd get caught surer 'n hell. But . . . you know. Show you how to work the problems. After school or lunch time." He waits for an answer and when none comes he stops grinning and begins cleaning his fingernails with a splinter he pulls off the bottom of the bench. "It's not hard after you get the hang of it."

"So they say."

In the gym behind the bleachers a bell rings and the boys stand and stretch before going down. Ryan is almost a head taller and much heavier in the chest and shoulders. Narrower hips. He watches Mole pick up his books and then he says, "How come you want to help me?"

Mole looks bewildered. Apparently a motive has not occurred to him and he can't think of one. "I don't know. Probably couldn't do you any good anyway. I just thought . . . you know . . . if college depends on that one course . . . well . . ." He trails off, and they walk down the bleachers.

As they pass the gym Ryan asks, "College mean that much to you?"

"Yeah. I mean, I guess so. Doesn't it to you?"

"I don't know. I can't think of any reason why I want

to go except to bug my old man. He doesn't think I can make it."

"Keeps you out of the army," says Mole.

"Probably the best reason. You been accepted already?"

"Stanford and Cal. Can't make up my mind which."

They go into the corridor of the main building and walk along past rows of lockers. Mole stops halfway down and begins twirling his combination. "What you got this period?" Ryan asks.

"English." Mole makes a face. "How 'bout you?"

"Biology. Listen. Are you serious about that geometry bit? Tutoring me, I mean?"

"Sure. Hell, yes. I'd be glad to."

"This afternoon?"

"Why not?"

"You want to take the books out to the beach and go over the homework?"

"Meet you in the parking lot by the gym."

By mid-November the weather is too cold to continue working out of doors and they move off the beach into Mole's house. The geometry comes easier. The work sessions get shorter and the bull sessions get longer. After a week Mole tells Ryan about his sexual escapades with various girls down on the beach. Ryan, who has a girl that he sees regularly, listens and keeps his mouth shut. After a second week Mole admits that his sexual escapades are fantasies; that the only women he has made have been whores. Ryan, whose girl has undergone a pregnancy scare and has broken off with him, smiles and listens and keeps his mouth shut. After a month Mole confesses that he is a virgin. Ryan grins and confesses that he is too.

By the time Cindy Blackburn, a buxom and much desired cheerleader, gives a New Year's Eve party and asks
Ryan to be her escort, the master-slave relationship is complete. But the master is beneficent. He gets Mole an invi-
tation to the party.

In front of the blackboard with a "Santa Cruz Unified
School District" label a man is still standing. He writes
problems on the board and retires behind his desk as
heads bend over exam books and pencils begin scratching.
The boy still sits and dreams of hot sand baking in the sun
. . . of Cindy Blackburn's hot, oiled body baking in the
sun . . . of surf pounding into the narrow opening of the
cove . . . of his Walter Mitty self pounding into the narrow
opening of Cindy Blackburn's hot, oiled body baking in
the sun. . . .

"Hey!" Mole whispers from behind his hand. "What are
you *doing*? Get going."

The boy shakes his head slightly, raises his eyebrows to
indicate hopeless despair. Begins to take perverse delight
at the thought of handing in a blank paper. To try and fail
would be an admission of stupidity. Better to ignore it and
admit indifference. But the good old Mole, who finishes
in half an hour, waits until the proctor turns to write a time
on the board, then hands his blue book across the aisle. In
the remaining twenty-five minutes Ryan earns an A-minus
in geometry and a place in the Freshman class on its way
to Stanford University. A tutorial triumph.

III

π Perhaps I'll make this a habit—this lawn lounging. Stretched out prone on my stomach I press my face into the thick grass and I can see into another world. I see back a hundred million years when things that crawled were kings on earth, when vegetation rioted out of the swamps and tidal ooze, and crept across the land, when the grasses swept over the continent and the first flower in a spring garden altered the face of the world. I see a tiny hard-shelled bug, warmed by the morning sun, come suddenly to life and begin a laborious passage through the forest of green. I give him an hour. Then something will eat him.

Once I knew a man who struggled an hour through the forest. Something was eating him, though he did not wait to be swallowed. He is a dead man now, but he visits me in occasional dreams. He helped himself to death. Even though darkness was just around the corner he could not wait. He saw no virtue in suffering when the end of suffering was a foregone conclusion. No one wrote him an obituary. His wife betrayed him just before he died. His body

was cremated and his ashes illegally tossed into the surf at
Point Lobos. He left nothing behind but a broken-down,
half-paid-for hotel on Tomales Bay, in which few people
ever stayed and which has now been torn down to make
room for a developer's marina.

His first name was Michael. The last name doesn't matter. Last names are nothing but unfortunate inheritances
from former failures. Last names mean family and family
means traditions of guilt and fear and hatred and Sunday
picnics with your cousins. Last names imply roots and
there are no roots in this land. The gophers eat them.

Michael had no roots. He was a free man and he lived as
he thought he ought to live. He died as he thought he
ought to die. He was never trapped by a tradition or a
myth. Alive, he was loved. Dead, he is forgotten—except
in occasional dreams where time does not matter. In
dreams his tiny bookstore still stands in its Santa Cruz alley near the Civic Auditorium. The fire that wiped him
out and drove him north to Tomales Bay has not yet been
set. The good citizen who burned his shop because it
smelled like beatnik has not yet been made irate by anon-
ymous letters to the local paper—letters about dirty books
and dirty people who sell them and dirty boys and girls
with dirty minds who buy them and spread dirt over the
clean and sterile playgrounds of our local high schools.

Mike was not dirty. He was not beat. He was not a
joiner or a rejecter. He washed and shaved and minded
his own business. But he had a half-Mexican, half-Indian
wife whose parents were fruit pickers. Perhaps Rosa
made the difference. Dirty brown skin.

That is your obituary, Michael. My gift to your memory
that haunts an occasional dream.

In those dreams your shop still stands, crammed with

paperbacks and art prints, weaving on the walls, a fretless banjo for sale behind the counter at the end—counter that never saw the light of day from under its load of papers, coffee cups, overflowing ashtrays, cashbox, posters for soon-to-appear rock 'n' roll bands, modern jazz quartets, folk singers, dance troupes, sitar players. Through the rear window the sun would pour into a bat-winged chair where a boy on his way to Stanford spent much of the summer playing a warn-out harmonica and watching the dust eddies swirl around his nest. It was his first rest home, his first sanitarium. Only there were people then, and there are no people now. Only probers. Healers. Mechanics of the mind.

Michael would say, "Why don't you get the hell out of here, Ryan, and quit wasting the day. Take a walk on the beach. Write a poem in the sand. Always sitting in here in the dark. . . ."

He would answer, "You sit in here in the dark."

And Michael would say, "I sit in this hole because it is my business. When I can get out, I get out. But you're on your way, old buddy, and I expect big things of you at the university. Get a head start, for crying out loud. Don't sit around on your butt blowing blues on a warped harmonica. Man, if I had your chance and your brains I wouldn't be making a living selling books."

"Some living. You give half of them away."

"If a guy wants to use his mind I should turn him off for a few pieces of silver?"

But Michael had it made. In his shop it was all soft and warm and idle. Rosa cooked tacos and enchiladas in the apartment over the store and brought them down with broken bits of crisp tortilla and a big pot of guacamole and we'd feed while she sat on a wood bench by the front door and practiced runs on her classical guitar. Gunboat Larson would come to town from a vineyard in Saratoga where he was acting as caretaker. A painter named Heckmann would come up from his cabin in Big Sur. Rosa's brother would come over from his picking job near Modesto, bring freshly cured marijuana, and we would all go out to the cove south of Santa Cruz and quietly get blasted watching the night surf pound the narrow strip of rocky beach.

Or we'd pile in the back of Gunboat's pickup truck and go down to Heckmann's cabin for a weekend of wine drinking and sun bathing. The back canyon where the cabin sat was almost tropical it was so lush with fern and wild morning glory and sphenopsids. Alders grew along the creek. A short, spongy moss covered the logs and stumps that lay everywhere in the woods. In the morning dew that collected on the platelike leaves of the nasturtium you could see the reflection of cloud and sky and a seabird drifting in a coastal updraft.

Michael would sit for hours on the rocks at the mouth of the canyon below the cabin, watching the foam patterns on the green swells. A decayed lump of rock stood offshore about fifty yards and when the sea was running big the spray would shoot high into the air and come apart at the top like an exploding sky rocket. At dusk the last rays of sunlight would catch in the foam as it burst and it would fall back like a meteor shower into the dark sea. No one could reach Michael then, not even Rosa. He would stay there on the rock until the night obscured everything around him before coming back up the trail to the cabin.

And always he was moody and quiet until supper was served.

In my dreams I see him still on his rock, watching the fireworks that moved him nearly to tears. Perhaps he sees his ashes drifting south along an icy current toward an ironic burial in the Tropic of Cancer. Finitude confronting infinity. Perhaps he saw it then, and wept for the impermanent season of his days.

Other ashes preceded his. From Soquel Avenue one mid-July night we watched the shop burn. For nearly three hours Michael stood with his hands in his pockets and watched the firemen play their hoses on the gutted and collapsing building. He didn't seem to care even how it had started and finally I asked a policeman. The cop questioned me for a while, checked my driver's license, took my name and address, and told me it looked like arson. A gasoline can had been found in the alley in front of the store. "Like whoever set it wanted us to know how it happened," he said.

Michael just shrugged and muttered. "Home of the vigilante. Home of the middle-class expatriate. Home of the illusion dwellers. Land of the free if you don't bug me. . . ." He studied his left thumb for a bit as if he thought it might reveal some truth, and then he sighed and said, "Come on, let's blow. It's all over. There is nothing left but the red tape and I don't guess I'll hang around for that."

We walked down Soquel Avenue toward Gunboat's pickup parked two blocks away. A dream walk. Slow motion, like we were up to our ankles in sand—or so it seems now. Gunboat and Rosa were in the truck, she crying, he chewing on a match, hunched down on the seat, glowering out the window. "What are you going to do?" I asked.

"Ah, me?" He opened the door and slid in next to his wife, put his arm around her shoulders and hugged her. He had a funny little smile on his face. "Me? I'm like the Phoenix bird, old buddy. I'll just rise up out of my own ashes and fly away."

He stuck his hand out the window and gave mine a shake. "I'll see you. Look me up at Gunboat's. If I'm not there he'll know where I've gone." Then the little smile faded away. "Listen, Ryan, get out of this town and quit fooling around. Quit hanging around with people who will only slow you down." Gunboat slammed the truck in low gear, rocketed down the street past a column of steamy smoke, turned left toward the mountains, and was gone.

The dream fades, dissolves in the wind, and is forgotten by its maker. Like the Phoenix it consumes itself in the fire of the morning sun. But when night begins to fall on Point Sur, and the last ray of light makes rainbows in the wind-driven spray, then will the dream rise again and proclaim its immortality.

IV

π A beachhead out of time. An interlude of surf and sand, fog and sun. Maybe it was the heat. Maybe the glare off the water or the incessant pound of the surf. Maybe I read too much Dostoevski. On a blazing afternoon in August I met myself. I lay in the sand and watched myself lie in the sand. Strange detachment. Ryan talked with Mole about girls and I listened to him with one ear and to the breakers with the other. I could hear his voice somewhere up in the top of my skull but I felt drowsy and feverish and only half attentive. Cloudless day without wind.

Mole is on his back with his arms crossed over his eyes, droning on about the women he desires. Who is speaking here? Who is listening? Confusing to be two, or three, or none at all. In the cove below my mother's house Mole pleads for love.

"Hey Ryan, when you going to fix me up with Cindy?"

"Too much woman for you, Mole."

"Man, would I like to get her back behind the break-water. Whooeee."

"Come off it Mole. Cindy'd take one look at your flabby ass and spring a leak."

Mole hums a little tune, digs in the sand with his feet, then rolls over and gets to his knees. He gathers his towel and slings it over his shoulder. "Gotta go. My Mom said that she'd nut me if I wasn't home by three."

"I'll bet she did. Yes sir, I can hear her saying it right now. 'Milton, I'm going to nut you if you aren't home by three.'" He rubs sand in Mole's hair. "Wonder is that she's not scared of crabs. She could lose a finger."

"You going to fix me up?"

"Hey listen, Moly. You know how you can get rid of them? Shave off one side and pour gasoline on the other. Get an ice pick and set fire to the hair."

"Your jokes are very old and they smell. Will you get me a date or no?"

"I mean it's sort of a social problem that must be crippling. You really should attend to it. Why don't you call her yourself?"

"Because I hardly know her and I'd have to explain who I am and all and it's embarrassing."

"How much is it worth to you?"

"Many thanks, friend. I spend two months teaching you the geometry you're too stupid to understand and . . ."

"Okay, okay. I'll fix you up."

"Good man. I'll see you later." And Mole sprints off across the sand, climbs up the narrow steps carved in the sandstone cliff, disappears over the rim, his towel flapping behind him.

The tide is out now and the gulls are down in the pools near the open end of the horseshoe cove. There is a strip of sand ten feet wide between the uppermost lick of the surf and the end of the rocks. It leads around onto the next beach. A girl is strolling through the passage, watching the gulls flap a few feet in the air and then settle down on their old perch after she goes by. Ryan, lying on his belly, cups his hand over his eyes. I watch him as he watches her coming up along the soft sand near the rocks. Tight blue elastic suit, respectably filled, long legs very tanned, and brown shoulders. Her hair is sun-bleached and cut short. Too far to tell about her face.

She moves along slowly, dragging her feet through the sand; past a blackened portion of the cliff where picnic fires have made a Rorschach test on the rock. Then suddenly she cries out, and spinning around, drops backward onto her behind, holding her right foot with both hands. It is not too far to see the blood. There is a great deal of it, and Ryan comes off his stomach and runs across to her. Her face shows pain but the first sting of the cut is gone and the real hurt will not begin until the shock has worn off.

"You must have hit a broken bottle or a can top," he says, looking at her foot. "People always leaving garbage." The slice seems clean but it is deep and it runs from behind her big toe down across her arch. It bleeds profusely. "Better get that to a doctor, quick. Probably need some stitches."

He helps her up and they hobble toward the steps on the other side of the cove. She has to ascend by herself, putting weight on the heel of her cut foot, and Ryan holds her under the arms from behind to steady her balance. She does not speak until they are in his car, speeding toward the Monroe Medical Plaza. "I'm getting blood on your car."

The sun has just dipped into the sea when Ryan and the girl leave Santa Cruz by the coast highway, headed for her home in La Honda. I float around in the car, observing. Every once in a while Ryan glances into the rear view mirror and catches my eye. I should have killed the bastard right there. He should have killed the bastard right there. Stopped the car and beat his head, my head, on the concrete until he, I, we went away and quit bugging me, him, us. But too much sun and I am dreamy. The sight of blood makes my head spin and disjoints my mind. Besides, it really is amusing to play the invisible man and watch myself . . . himself . . . ourselves . . . and the girl. One and one make three? Or is it one and one and one make two?

The girl's name is Ellen and she is a student at Stanford when it isn't summer. Her father is dead, killed in a wreck on the Peninsula side of the La Honda road, and her mother lives alone in San Francisco. Ellen uses the old house in La Honda when she feels like it. She tells us this in a groggy, low-pitched voice. The doctor has given her something for pain and shock and she is only half alive.

"I'm sorry to put you to all this," she says, as her head rolls on the back of the seat.

"It's no trouble. What better way to meet a good-looking girl in a bathing suit?"

"I can think of a few," she mumbles and then seems to pass into sleep.

And she is pretty. Not unusual, or striking, or exotic. Her features are all perfectly normal. Straight nose that is neither too big nor too small, full mouth and a round, well-formed chin, wide-spaced eyes, small ears, clear skin, and soft blond hair. All normal, all correct. A normal, correct face. The kind of features that win beauty contests because they add up to a Madison Avenue image of healthy good looks.

Ryan turns off the coast road at San Gregorio and drives inland through dusk and fog until the road begins to curve into a canyon of redwood and starts a gradual ascent into the foothills. But back up a minute. Back to the flat part where the oaks are standing around in the open pastures, *weeping*. Why are they so *sad*? Why have I never noticed before that they are so tragic and so ominous? Their faces are drawn down in masks of despair and the one over there with the broken limb writhes with the pain of his wound. *Danse Macabre* is no *fantasy*. But no matter. Ryan is in the foothills, in the redwoods, and I haven't time to get hung up. He leans over and shakes the girl awake. "Hey, Ellen. Come to. You've got to show me where you live."

She motions him to stop at a sign proclaiming "Redwood Terrace" and he hooks a U-turn onto a narrow paved road that looks as if it had been under a constant mortar barrage since the day of its construction. A quarter mile of jolts and bumps and she indicates a low yellow house beneath a tall stand of trees. Ryan pulls through the collapsing stone pillars that were once somebody's idea of how to make a summer cabin look like an estate. He helps her into the living room and on to the couch and then goes back for her beach towel and newly acquired crutches.

"This is some place," he says, propping the crutches behind the sofa.

"Nice when there's sun. Mostly it's damp and gloomy, but I like it."

"Me too," Ryan says. "It's a great gas. Sort of Waldenish, you know? With the trees and bushes growing up against the windows. Like living in a Rousseau painting."

She stretches out on the couch and puts her bandaged foot on a pillow. She takes a cigarette off the coffee table and he lights it for her.

"The guy who owned it before my father," she says, "had all kinds of crazy pagodas and connected pools and little nooks and gardens and fountains with abalone shells encrusted around their edges. Lights hidden behind the shells, all kinds of weird scenes. Every time I go out I find a new piece of pipe sticking out of the ground that doesn't seem to come from anywhere or go to anyplace. It's really nutty, but it's quiet and it's mine."

"You stay out here all summer?"

"Usually. I even come out weekends when school is on. Sign out to my mother's and just come out here and paint or lie around. There's nobody to bother me. You know, in town you go to the bathroom or something and you always have to close the curtains because some jerk in the next cheesebox over is trying to peek in. I really go nuts in town."

"Speaking of town," Ryan says, "I'd better get going. I'll have to come back and see this place in the daylight sometime."

"Please do. Come back and I'll cook you a steak. I owe you a great deal."

"No, nothing. Listen, your car's still down at the cove, I guess. Unless you walked thirty-five miles."

"My God, I forgot all about it."

"I'll get a friend of mine and bring it up on Saturday. Nothing else to do." He ignores her protests. "Saturday. You sure you're going to be all right here?"

"Yes. Thanks."

Driving back from La Honda on Saturday night, Ryan flips on the windshield wipers to clear off the heavy mist that keeps collecting. Full of steak and beer. Rhythm and blues station coming in from Oakland. The damp air seems to deaden all sounds of wind and road and inside the car it is warm and quiet except for the music. Mole is beside himself. Ecstatic. He keeps shaking his head and pulling his hand down over his face. "Man, oh man, what a doll. What an absolute doll. What a figure. What a face. And nice, bright as hell, fantastic. And she goes to Stanford and I'm going to Stanford and you're going to Stanford and we're all going to Stanford. Oh Christ, what a broad."

"Now we're even for the geometry, Mole buddy. Paid in full. A pie for a pi. I sell only first-line merchandise."

"Hey Ryan, do you really think I can make out with a chick like that? I mean, she must have fifty guys sniffing around her doorstep."

"I didn't see any there tonight. Did you?"

"Yeah. Us. Anyway, how am I going to work it to go back up there and see her again?"

"Well, Mole, I don't know. Just go. Go up there and say 'I liked you so I came back for seconds.' What you want a phony reason for? You're set up. You want it plugged in for you too?"

"No. But just waltzing in some afternoon isn't my style. I've got to have a reason."

"I wouldn't worry about violating your style, buddy. It won't be hurting much."

They drive in silence past the Pigeon Point lighthouse, and a few miles farther, when the coastline swings in toward the southeast, they are out of the mist. The full moon hangs just outside the window on Mole's side of the car. Bright V of light across the black sea and a ghostly line of surf shimmering along pale beaches.

"Look. That MG of hers is about to throw a rod. Call and ask her if she'd like it fixed. Tell her you've got a whole backyard full of MG parts."

"Hey, that's not bad. Yeah. Very groovy idea. Only you have to help me. I don't know from nothing about any MG."

Ryan looks across at Mole. Shaking his head he steps down heavily on the gas pedal and races the moon into Santa Cruz.

Sing again, "All the good times are past and gone." The interlude fades like a summer's tan. Clip the roots once more. They don't go so deep. Pack the associations and move on. Go west, young man, go west. And if you can't go west go north. Go north to college and get an education. And when that's over? When you've used up all the directions and run as far and as fast as you can and there's no place to go because you've been there? Well . . . just sit down . . . young man . . . and take a weary look up and down that long lonesome road. And then . . . after that? Well . . . who can say?

PART THREE

I

π Doctor Vickery told me this morning that he needs a vacation. He wants to escape, he says, to somewhere that is quiet and deserted—a place where he can relax and forget the world for a while. I told him I would take him to Tomales Bay. And I told him it wouldn't help. There is no escape.

In the early morning there is a glassy stillness on Tomales Bay. Vapor rises slowly off the water and the dawn is filtered through a misty blanket of dispersing fog. A salmon boat glides through the murky light toward Bodega Head and the Pacific Ocean, and across the still water the low green cliffs of the Point Reyes peninsula are just beginning to emerge from under a glaucous layer of cloud. A flock of sanderlings dart past, the pale light flashing off their white underwings as they swoop and veer in an erratic series of maneuvers. From a marsh near where I stand an American egret lifts heavily from his shallow perch, soars for a graceful moment over the pebbled beach, and sits down again in his old place. Pink with the plumage of dawn, he regards me warily and stalks deeper into the tangled reeds toward shore. Three miles west, across the uplands that are now visible over the cliffs, the Pacific surf pounds on fifteen miles of Point Reyes rocks and beach, sending up a muffled roar so constant in volume and pitch that its drone becomes almost unnoticeable.

A log and plank pier juts out from Michael's newly acquired old Victorian hotel that is built half on the land and half over the water. Dilapidated building. Gray-green paint, faded and turned to chalk. Shingles stained from the rusty plumbing pipes that poke up out of the roof. Ryan stands with me on the pier. I stand with Ryan on the pier. The sun is at our backs. A single shadow falls on the boards.

The door off the hotel dining room opens and Ellen comes out wearing slacks and tennis shoes and a heavy wool sweater. She stands for a moment looking across the bay and then walks along the pier. "Hi."

"Where's Mole?"

"Still getting dressed. He's such a slowpoke."

They walk out to a small shack at the end of the pier where Michael keeps his fishing gear and outboard motors. Ellen sits down on the planks and swings her feet over the water. "You going with us today? Mike said we can use the boat."

"Collecting more limpets?"

"We thought we might hunt abalone, too. Why don't you come? You know how Mole is when he's 'researching.' I'm left with nobody to talk to."

"I'd like to but I have my own paper to write. Due last week."

"Stick-in-the-mud." She twists around, still swinging her feet, and grimaces at him. "Boy, am I glad I graduated. No more papers, no more exams. Just life and freedom and my two lovers."

"Mole and who?"

"You, love. Everywhere you go, we go."

"Not quite. I still manage to keep a private bedroom."

Laughing again, she rocks clear over on her back and looks at him upside down. "I'll speak to Milt about it."

"I don't think a threesome is his game."

Ellen continues to lie on the planks, her eyes closed and a light wind ruffling her hair. Ryan hunches down against the shack, picks between his front teeth with a fishhook, and watches her. I watch them both. I think she must be happy, in a mindless way. Takes what comes along and follows her whims—as far as her father's insurance money will let her. But lovely. Very lovely, I think now. Maybe you were a fool, Ryan, to give the best portion to your buddy. Maybe you should take it back. Pale cheeks, paler waters where'er I sail. Paler than yours, Ahab.

Mole and Ellen are gone. The faint sound of their motor drifts across the quiet bay. Ryan helps Michael flush out one of his motors in a barrel of fresh water and they put it back on its rack in the shed. For a few moments they stand watching a catamaran skim along the bay and then they turn and go into the hotel for coffee.

"I've got to go into Petaluma for a few hours, Ryan. You going to be around the hotel?"

"Yes."

"You mind keeping an eye on things? Anybody shows up just rent them a room. There's a rate card somewhere in the desk. If you can't find it just charge whatever the hell you feel like. Rosa just left for her mother's for the week so the place is yours."

"Take your time."

Ryan settles down in what once was the hotel ballroom, now full of overstuffed couches and chairs and stand-up lamps with colored glass shades. A grandfather clock tocks hollowly in the corner and the water laps against the pilings under the floor. He stretches out on a faded plush couch, props his head on the collapsing arm, and opens his book.

> Complacencies of the peignoir, and late
> Coffee and oranges in a sunny chair,
> And the green freedom of a cockatoo
> Upon a rug mingle to dissipate
> The holy hush of ancient sacrifice.
> She dreams a little, and she feels the dark
> Encroachment of that old catastrophe
> As a calm darkens among water-lights.

The clock marks the beat. Lap, lap, lap, under the floor. He dreams a little. Jerks awake. Makes a note in the margin. *Poem begins and ends with bird image.* Continues on. Loses his place.

> The pungent oranges and bright, green wings
> Seem things in some procession of the dead,
> Winding across wide water, without sound.
> The day is like wide water, without sound.

Far, far in the distance a boy stands on a lawn tossing a ball into the air. Catching and tossing, catching and tossing, catching and tossing. Running now, running. Running across wide water without sound, running across water, without sound, running. . . .

"You get a lot of work done?"

Ryan opens his eyes. Michael stands in the door holding a whole salmon in one hand and a half gallon of burgundy in the other. "Wake up, pal. It's quarter to five."

"Jesus. I must have slept all afternoon."

"Your buddy and his girl are still out. Boat's not here anyway. How you feel about salmon for supper?"

On the deck behind the kitchen Ryan dumps charcoal into a double hibachi, pours kerosene on it, and sets it on fire. While they wait for coals they drink half of the bottle of burgundy. Across the bay the cliffs are in purple twilight. A salmon boat chugs back down the dark bay toward its mooring at the Marshal Boat Works, and from the deserted feed and grain barn next to the hotel the bats are beginning to drop from their crevices and out through the loft window. They flit across the violet sky.

"You think that guy is going to make it back?" Michael says.

"Probably."

"What's his scene with the girl?"

"Who knows? They been going together two or three years. I guess he'd like to marry her, but she's in no rush. Something like that."

Michael takes a filleted half of the salmon, brushes garlic butter over the pink meat, and flops it on the grill. "I think it's like she's got it for you."

"Maybe."

Michael looks across the hibachi at him. Rubs his finger under his nose a few times. "You're a strange bird, old buddy. A strange bird. And I think you're wasting."

"Pass the jug."

They eat in near darkness. Only the light from the kitchen window shines over the deck. When Ryan finishes he goes to the railing and tosses the scraps from his plate out into the water and goes inside. Michael carries the plates and glasses into the sink and together they do the dishes. In the living room an elderly couple sits playing dominoes and the night is soft and quiet.

"What do you say we go out on the pier and blow a little grass," Michael says. "See if they show up."

"What time is it?"

"Nine-thirty."

"He probably hit a rock and sank. He's not too handy with anything that has a motor in it. Can't drive a car in a straight line for fifty feet."

Michael takes a flashlight out of a closet in the lobby and they go out the dining room door and along the pier. In the shed Ryan holds the light while Michael rolls a joint, tapping the shredded weed out of a matchbox into a double thickness of Zig-Zag paper. He licks the seam, twists the end, wets it, and holds it to the flame of his lighter. Blowing out the burning paper, he hands it to Ryan. "Let's sit outside."

"Wide water without sound."

"Huh?"

"A poem."

They dangle their feet over the edge of the planks and there is no sound but the *soop soop* as they breathe their tokes and pass the joint back and forth. When it is too short to handle Ryan butts it, takes a cigarette and rolls the tobacco out of the end, and puts the roach in the empty paper. He lights it, breathes in, and passes it "Sweet gage," he says, expelling his breath. "I'm stoned."

"I'm a wee bit zonked myself," Michael says. And then after a bit, "How you making out at the university? You pulling your weight?"

"I'm . . . slitherin' on by."

"Ah, you can do more than that, ducky. I got faith. I got faith . . ."

Shortly after ten there are voices out on the water and the sound of oars creaking in their locks. Lying on his back Ryan floats mindlessly and watches the stars. Dreamy, quiet. He considers the sound for a while. No hurry. How long have I heard them now? Must be twenty minutes. Ten at least. Don't seem much closer. I wish every weed in the world was pot. "Hey Michael. Am I just high or is that somebody punting on the Thames?"

"Man, I believe it's the *Queen Mary*." He sits up and flashes the light out into the blackness. Shouts. Mole's voice, and Ellen's. Oars creaking in rusty locks. After a hundred years they pull up alongside the pier and moor the boat. "What is it? What? Motor quit? Rowed all the way home? Holy shit! Hey Ryan, this cat's rowed five and a half miles. Yeah, sure. By all means. Kitchen's full of chow. Help yourself. Be in in a minute. Put the motor away. C'mon, Ryan, gimme a hand with this."

They haul the motor out of the boat and drag it into the shed. Ryan holds the light as Michael hoists it onto the rack and screws down the clamps. "Lessee what he's done to my bird here." He takes the light and shines it on the controls, fiddles with a knob, seems to take forever, rubber thumbs, begins to chuckle. Infectious pot laughter. Ryan chuckles too, not sure why. Michael starting to break up, Ryan convulsed. They lean against the wall of the shed with tears running down their faces, howling at nothing in particular—their own mirth, their own idiocy —out of control. They wheeze and gasp and ache and cry. Then it's over. Michael turns the knob counterclockwise as far as it will go. "Your buddy had the choke on full. Flooded the engine. Let's go get something to drink."

II

π In the early morning there is a glassy stillness on Tomales Bay. Vapor rises off the water; curls around a salmon boat that glides out toward Bodega Head. The cliffs across the water begin to fade into the picture. Weak solution. Need more developer. Get it right and print a hundred copies. Ryan is still with me on the pier. Shadowless. Always standing directly in front.

The door off the hotel dining room opens and Ellen comes out wearing black tights and a black turtleneck made of stretch fabric. Hips and thighs faintly white under the taut fabric. She carries a glass of Scotch in her hand and her blond hair bursts suddenly like a flash bulb in a dark room. Spots in front of my eyes. Where have I seen this before? Strange that she makes no sound as she walks. Why didn't she close the door? My eyeballs are seared out of their sockets. Cover them with my hands and shut out the light.

"Hey stupid. Don't you know any better than to look

right into the sun?" Mole comes out to the end of the pier
and squats down by the shed, next to Ryan. "What's the
matter? You sick?"

"No. Nothing's the matter. Where's Ellen?"

"Still in bed. Pooped after last night."

"Still in bed?"

"Yeah. Say, what's with you anyway? You sure
you're . . ."

"I'm fine."

Mole stretches out on the planks and suns himself like a
great seal. "This is a cool place, Ryan. I've been looking
over the history of Point Reyes. . . ." Chamber of com-
merce guidebook. Mole's endless fund of information
about everything and every place and everybody on earth.
His voice becomes a disembodied noise that hums around
Ryan's ears. ". . . middle of the bay . . . tremendous earth-
quake fault . . . San Andreas and the bay . . . fault depression. . . . Five hundred years ago . . . than there are now.
In fact, anthropologists have found . . . over on the Point
Reyes peninsula . . . for centuries before the Spanish occupied the region. You listening, Ryan?"

"I'm listening."

"The Miwoks were really a scene, you know? Ran
around in the fog practically naked, freezing their butts
off, living in crude huts. Never minded it. Fished with
spears. Hunted with them too."

"I thought they probably had shotguns, Mole."

"Yeah. Ha Ha. Shotguns. They were really . . . until the
Spanish showed up . . . started proselytizing. Got them
all . . . for about thirty years. Then the Franciscans split
and the Indians couldn't remember how to do anything
and they . . . . That's how it is. Along comes Jesus and
everybody croaks."

The dining room door slams and Ellen comes out wearing slacks and tennis shoes and a heavy wool sweater. She walks along the pier to the end and hops up on an empty oil drum by the shed. Inhales deeply to show she likes the morning.

"How'd you sleep?" Mole asks.

"Great."

"Ryan and I have just been having a monologue. You still feel like driving around Point Reyes today?"

"Unhuh." She takes another deep breath. "What a great morning."

"You going to come with us today, Rye?" Mole asks.

"I guess. Sure, why not?"

Mole stands up and goes over to Ellen. Takes her hand. She slides off the drum and kicks Ryan in the hip. "Come on, lazy man. Mike was in the kitchen when I came down. Let's get something to eat."

They drive down the eastern side of the bay to Point Reyes Station and then back up the west side to Inverness. Mole buys a can of sardines and a loaf of bread, chocolate bars, some Monterey Jack cheese, and a fifth of cheap red wine. Throws it all into a rucksack in the back of the car. They follow the road back to the recently built park headquarters at Bear Valley. From there they walk.

There is haze over the moon here. I remember vaguely. Mole bounding ahead, bounding back, running up a little side trail, running back. Pointing out a tree, a flower, a rock formation. Saying there are three hundred kinds of birds in the park. An old logging road leads through forests of Bishop pine, Douglas fir. Higher up there are open meadows with madrones and oaks. We eat lunch at some point where we look down on Drake's Bay and Mole continues his morning monologue. "In 1597 Sir Francis Drake put into the natural harbor down there at the southern end of the peninsula to make repairs on the *Golden Hind.* . . ."

There is a trail along Inverness Ridge that brings us to the foot of Mount Wittenburg and Mole insists on climbing it. We wait for him and lie in the tall grass of a small meadow near the path. Ellen asks, "What are you going to do after this year? After you finish your B.A.?"

"Don't know. Go on, maybe." Ryan rolls over on his stomach, takes out a cigarette and lights it. "How about you? You and Mole going to get married?"

"Oh, I don't know." She waves her hand, dismissing the question, and they lie in the sun without talking. After a while she says, "Ryan, can I ask you a question?"

"Shoot."

"You remember when I first met you, three years ago? On the beach. And you took me home with that cut foot."

"I remember."

"Well, I always sort of wondered. When you came back a few days later with Milt, it was sort of as if you were shoving me on him. Or him on me. I don't know. Just a feeling." She paused. "Can I have a cigarette?"

"I wasn't shoving anybody."

"Oh, I know. It's just silly. A feeling I had." She drags on the cigarette. "But, I always sort of wondered . . . you know . . . why you never took me out yourself."

"Do you love Mole?"

Another pause. "I guess."

"Well, there's your answer."

"Not exactly."

"It'll suffice."

They go on smoking and the meadow is quiet except for the drone of an occasional insect. When Ryan has snuffed his butt and is lying back on the grass with his hands behind his head, Ellen leans over, suddenly, and kisses him. He leaves his eyes open and his hands where they are. From the path above Mole halloos. "Come on. Let's roll." Perhaps he has not seen.

"You are a strange bird," Ellen says.

In the car Mole is less vocal. Perhaps his hike up Mount Wittenburg has worn him out. Still, he insists on driving out to the Point Reyes lighthouse and he urges Ryan to hurry before the sun sets.

The road is narrow and winding. It climbs from Tomales Bay up over the Inverness Ridge and then out along the treeless and windswept western promontory, past Schooner Bay, past the overgrown graveyard of eight or ten coast guard sailors lost in rescue operations off the point. The grave markings are faint and the tilting stones are surrounded by a pale, weathered white fence. They pass the RCA transmitting and receiving station, and drive across moorlike grazing land until they come finally to the sheer cliffs at land's end. Ellen is tired and stays in the car. Ryan and Mole walk along the rocky path toward the lighthouse compound. Mole is still silent. When they reach the final precipice and stand looking almost straight down at the boiling green and white and black Pacific, he manages to speak.

"Hey old buddy. What's it between you and Ellen? Am I getting bird-dogged?"

"No. There's nothing. And don't be so goddamned jolly about it. Just say what's bugging you straight out and never mind being cute."

"That's about the longest speech I've ever heard you make." Mole chuckles.

Ryan does not smile. He looks away at the little flight of worn wooden steps that lead a hundred yards down the rock to the light at the sea's edge.

"Well, okay," Mole says. "I've known you too long and like you too well to play games. I guess I'm just upset because I came down from Wittenburg a little too soon."

"A little too late, don't you mean?"

"I guess. You know how I am about Ellen, and if there's something going on, I'd like to know about it."

"You saw her kiss me."

"Yes."

"I can't explain that. Just forget it."

Mole looks at him for a minute, then shrugs. He turns and starts to walk back to the car alone.

The surf explodes on the jagged rocks and cliffs below, sending sheets of white water fifty, seventy, a hundred feet into the air. The wind rips at Ryan's hair and clothes, and a heavy mist from the drifting spray blasts him in the face. In the twilight gloom he leans against the thin cable guardrail and looks out over two thousand miles of empty black water.

III

π I am getting nowhere. The demons of the past don't seem to be acquainted with the demons of the present. There is always a sense of *déjà vu* when I let my imagination out of its cage, but I can't quite pin down the pattern and it is becoming a tiresome game. Pinball lobotomy. Fire my mind at an image and watch it bounce off little rubber-ringed posts while lights and bells flash and clang in the background, until finally it drops into a small black hole and disappears. Try to control it and it tilts.

A hawk circled over today while I was lying on the lawn, and I thought, "Take me with you, bird." If Keats can do it so can I. Take me home to the coast. To Santa Barbara or Monterey or Santa Cruz. Fly me to Partington Ridge and let me look out over the Big Sur at dawn, before the fog has burned away and an endless expanse of cotton fluff floats over the sea. Let me soar out over the headlands and look back at the soft brows of the mountains pushing out into the ocean like a great leviathan herd drifting southwest in the current. Let me sit and watch the surf batter the jagged rocks that encrust an emerald coast. Long streamers of neon hair wave out from the sea stacks when the swells roll in. The water that boils inland past the reefs is heavily marbled with foam.

When I begin to smell salt in the air the hawk changes his shape, turns from brown to white with tips of gray. The brightness in his eye dulls and I perceive that he is nothing but an old gull, wearily cruising over the combers just north of Santa Cruz. At least he has brought me back. There is film in his faded pink eyes and he is nearly blind. Exhausted, he settles down on an outcropping of rock between the highway and the sea, and stands there, motionless, sick, head pulled in on his breast.

I lend him my eyes. One stares at the ghost of an oil tanker sliding down the gray horizon; the other gazes obliquely back at a deep canyon that empties onto the beach. A long, high bridge spans the canyon and a creek flows at the bottom, nearly dry. Beyond the bridge the road curves sharply between low dunes and there is a yellow sign that indicates a dangerous curve. Double line on the asphalt. Only wooden posts and an eight-inch strip of metal between the careful and the dead.

The gull sits motionless and the wind blows sand across the road. From where he is perched I can see over the dunes and down the highway that stretches south along the coast. Fields run to the lip of the land where the cliffs fall straight into the sea. An old white barn, faded and collapsing, and a Holstein cow munching thistles in the yard of some Portuguese farmer who scrapes his life out of the rich black soil behind the ragged and always crumbling headlands.

I hear a low, steady whine before I see the sports car, running hot and fast through the distant artichoke fields. Then it pops over a hill into sight and tears along in the fading afternoon toward a poppyflower sun drowning in the offshore bank of mist.

I recognize the car and its driver. I rebuilt them both. To one I gave Ellen, and to the other, new rings, valves, and pistons. How long ago? I can't remember. A thousand years past. Back when we were in college. Perhaps before. But I am an Indian-giver. I took Ellen back, though Mole never knew it. The car I left in the bottom of the canyon where Mole reduced it and himself to twisted scrap. When I got drunk enough one afternoon to go and look, somebody had stolen the seats and instruments. Even the wheel.

Sand blows softly on the road. Vanilla swirls in a marble cake. The wind ruffles the gull's tail feathers as it stands watching the sun grow smaller and the car grow larger. It is almost to the dilapidated barn now, and the cow stops gumming her thistles and watches it flash by, its pipes rattling off the windows of the farmer's house. When the echo fades the cow begins chewing again.

There is no top on the MG and I see my old tan cowboy hat perched on Mole's head. Last remnant of a southwestern prep school. The starch has long since gone out of the brim and he has one side pinned up like an Australian hunter. Very dapper. Yellow garter for a band, won in a penny arcade shooting gallery on the Santa Cruz boardwalk. 'What'll it be, boys? A Kewpie doll, or this beautiful band for your best girl's leg?" A groovy addition for your lid, Mole. Yellow like the sign that flashes past as the car blasts into the dunes. Its speed, if anything, increases.

The tires begin a protesting whine as Mole guides his machine around the last low hill. He makes it through the curve and shoots out onto the bridge but the stress is finally too much. The rear wheels break loose from the sand-blown road and the scream of rubber on asphalt becomes a shrieking skid that sends the gull straight up into the air. Mole frantically cramps the wheel away from his slide. As he is about to slam into the left guardrail, the tires catch and the car snaps around. The steering wheel spins back like a propeller, its spokes breaking Mole's fingers like matchsticks. Three hundred and thirty degrees. Almost full around. Smoking, howling rubber rips off on the rough pavement and then the front end smashes through the posts and snaps the steel band like old string. The impact separates the driver from his vehicle. As the one falls down along the center girder of the bridge, the other flails wildly out in a prolonged, descending arc, bounces off a sandstone boulder, and drops into the creek. The Australian hunter's hat held by the chin strap is still intact, but its crown is turning from tan to rust and the yellow band is becoming sticky.

The gull has not seen this. When the howl of the tires first interrupts the tranquillity of soft wind and surf he escapes, squawking along the beach in search of a more protected perch. But I stay with my head-splitting dreams, watching the pinball bounce back and forth across the boards, racking up a greater and greater score and more and more free games. I stay and wait, and from under a pile of twisted metal near the mouth of the canyon, I hear the radio playing into the empty night. Rhythm and blues.

IV

π In her house in La Honda we wait, listening to Coltrane and Jimmy Giuffre recordings while the redwoods gather in the fog and wring it out on the roof. Pat . . . pat . . . pat . . . gentle backdrop to the music, sometimes right with the beat. There are candles burning in green wine bottles even though it is not quite dark outside, and Ellen's not-so-good paintings hang on the walls. The mist swirls in and out of the trees and licks across the windows. Foliage damp and glistening like wax.

The changer clicks and the cool trip is suddenly shattered by Clark Terry and Art Blakey driving through a wild version of "Swahili." Old EmArcy disc with a scratch across side one. Blakey's drums are primitive and erotic.

"Mole should be here any time," I say.

"He should have been here an hour ago."

My back prickles with the dry heat of a sunburn and I ask her to rub Sea and Ski into it while I sit like Buddha on a big satin pillow in front of the speakers and sway with Terry's wild horn. She bends over behind me and the beach robe she wears over her bikini falls open as she works the oily lotion around my shoulders. When she is done I turn around and kiss her navel. "When are you and Mole gonna get married?"

"That's kind of a *non sequitur*, isn't it?"

"Huh?"

"Do you always kiss women below the belt and then ask when they are getting married?"

She puts the Sea and Ski on the table, wipes her hands on the robe, and smooths back her short blond hair. With her arms raised her robe is wide open and I'm gaping at her long legs and pointed breasts. In the candle light the hairs on her thighs look like a soft golden down. "I can do better than kiss your navel."

"The mole and the anteater," she says and laughs, and suddenly my stomach is on fire and I'm hoping that Mole won't show up tonight.

"That's a pretty risqué metaphor for you, Drucilla," I say. "Hardly your customary line."

She flops back on the couch and pulls her legs up under her chin, holding them around with her arms, so that I'm looking into the soft bulge of a buttock, blue veined under the tan and cut in half by the elastic of her suit. The bottoms of her feet and toes are dirty. "You have a capacity for bringing out the worst in me, Ryan."

"Do I?"

"Yes. In fact, you make me very nervous. I get very self-conscious when you're around."

"Izzat so?"

As if to prove it she lights a cigarette and puts it in the ashtray, picks up the Sea and Ski and begins rubbing it into her legs.

"Yes," she says. "That's so."

"Well, I find you very relaxing, so we make a pair."

"You find everybody relaxing, Ryan. I think that's because you're never really aware that anyone else is around."

"Hey, I should be on the couch. I'll get you your note pad, doctor, and we can begin this in earnest."

She gets off the couch and walks around my pillow to the changer. The record has stopped and she flips it over, searching the titles on side two, then sets it back down and pushes the button. A short piano introduction, chords piling up to an unresolved line, then Dinah Washington's saxophone voice, "Love . . . for sale. Advertising young love . . . for sale."

"You do that on purpose?" I joke.

She stands looking at me for a bit, unsmiling as if her mind is somewhere else. And then she says, "It's never for sale." She relights the cigarette that has gone out in the ashtray and sits back down on the couch. We listen to the record clear through without talking. When it is over I put on another one.

"I wonder where Milt is," she finally says. "He's always late, but not this late."

"He said if he wasn't here by ten he wouldn't make it."

"I should think he'd call. Unless more of you has rubbed off on him than I think."

"You never answered my original question about getting married."

"I'm sorry. Did you propose? I was listening to the music."

"Okay, okay, so we'll drop the subject."

"I don't know, Ryan. I don't know if we are. We've talked about it, that's all. You want to hear a wanton admission? I feel a lot more sure of how I feel about Milt when you stay locked up inside yourself. That's not very nice, is it? Not a very firm basis on which to go to the altar."

She's started it in me again. Building little bonfires. And we look at each other and *know* what is going to happen. So is it my fault?

"We can tell from the bedroom if anybody comes."

"You know, Ryan, I'm awfully glad that I don't have you for a best friend."

"I can assure you, he'd do the same for me," I say, and as I roll off my cushion and start walking on my knees toward her, lights flash across the windows that face the drive and a car pulls up.

"I doubt if he would," she says, and disappears into the bedroom to change out of her suit.

But the driver has made a mistake, and when he discovers his blunder he begins backing out. The lights flash again across the windows and I hear the clash of gears as he shifts too quickly from reverse to low. "Grind me a pound, touch hole." I realize that the record player is silent . . . has been silent . . . and in a curious ambivalence of anger and relief over the intruding car I walk over and put on John Lewis' "Improvised Meditations and Excursions." A Charlie Parker tune, "Now's the Time." Single piano notes and a chord. Bahm. Bass working up and down behind the melody. Ba Ba Ba BABA Ba. I lie back on the floor and turn up the volume.

"Is it Milt?" she calls over the music. Never calls him Mole. I wonder why? Suddenly I'm aching in the groin again as I catch her through the open bedroom door going from bathroom to dresser in a bra and panties no more

ample than her swimming suit. Pale and transparent as
my mind.

"No. Some idiot looking for a place to screw his chick."

"The woods seems to be full of them, huh Ryan." This
time she laughs. "If you want a drink there's some bourbon in the cupboard. I don't know what else."

"I can't stand bourbon. If I smell the cork I get sick.
Had a bad time on it once."

"Well, there may be some Scotch. Pour me something,
will you?" And she goes back into the bathroom.

I'm cracking ice cubes out of the tray and thinking that
maybe she's putting in her diaphragm when suddenly it
hits me that this is Mole's girl, Mole's future wife maybe,
and that I am the one who turned them onto each other.
I'm the third man theme. I towed them around in my
wake for two years. I'm the advisor, the consultant. I
bought Mole Bloody Marys for breakfast when he came
back one morning with his virginity gone. I calmed him
down when he thought she was pregnant. I found an ask-
no-questions doctor in San Jose to give her overdoses of
estrogen in case she really was. I'm like their priest, for
Christ's sake, and here I am, Ryan the best-buddy, standing with my hands under the windowsill straining upward
with all my might trying to get rid of a case of lover's
nuts for my best friend's girl and all the time I'm hoping
that Mole has run his car into a tree or something and
won't make it tonight.

But the guilt is not all mine. Not all mine. When she
comes out of the bathroom she is wearing black tights and
a sleeveless black turtleneck made of stretch fabric, and
when she walks over to take the Scotch I have poured for

her my mind collapses like a pricked balloon. I see only her hips and thighs faintly white under the taut fabric and the shadow outline of hard nipples under her shirt. And we are completely lost. It's well after ten and Mole will not be here. My stomach is jelly. We stand in the kitchen facing each other, sipping our drinks and saying nothing, swaying with the music, unblinking masks of lust, smiles of idiocy. Ten minutes . . . fifteen maybe, until she looks down at the front of the swimming trunks that I am still wearing and sees what I'm not trying to conceal or repress, and I put my glass down and pull her toward me, running my hands up and down her back and over her firm buttocks, and then slip my hands inside her tights and peel them down below her soft, grinding hips.

A high concrete bridge carries the coast road over a rocky canyon. A creek runs at the bottom, nearly dry . . . faintly red. Double lines on the asphalt; frail posts and metal between the careful and the dead; blood-washed moon over a shrouded sea. Mist swirls around the towering pillars of the bridge and a radio plays rhythm and blues over the dark and empty beach.

V

π Ellen is sleeping on her stomach. The sheet is down around her hips and there is a golden stripe of sunlight across her back. I inch up toward the headboard until the light falls over my chest and drips off the edge of the bed onto the floor. I lie staring at one of her paintings on the opposite wall, a view from Sausalito across the bay to San Francisco. Hazy violet shadows of buildings and hills, blue-gray water, and in the foreground two sailboats, a ketch and a small schooner I think, moored at a rickety wooden pier. Somehow she has not quite gotten the right perspective. San Francisco looks as if it were across a lake instead of the whole expanse of the bay. But the boats are good. Masts and spars and rigging swaying against the sky.

From the picture in the box I had tried to imagine how it would look when I finished it. An 880-ton bark heeling to port, or was it starboard, in a heavy gale that blew out of the artist's imagination. The bowsprit is almost in the water and the deck lies over conveniently so that the hatches and cabins can be seen from the top. "This kit contains machine-carved hull block, shaped from selected wood." Smooth the hull, the deck, the bulwarks. Use various grades of garnet paper. Check your materials: keel, stem, rudder post, channels, rubbing strakes, rails, stanchion rails, pin rails, bumpkin rails, fife rails.

"Ryan, what time is it?"

Catheads, and bitts, after cabin, forward cabin, for'd hatch. Why do they abbreviate one and spell the other? Wheel house, coach house, sundries and extras.

"Hey."

"What?"

"It must be getting late. What time is it?"

"I don't know. Your painting reminds me of a model ship I once spent about ten years trying to build."

She rolls over and sits up, pulling the sheet around her waist and wrapping it around behind her. Pink-tipped breasts, golden-striped with sun. "Ryan, it must be late. Will you get up and get out of here before I start to think about what we've done and get depressed."

"If I'm gone you won't think about it?"

"I'll think about it, but I won't have to look at it. You might at least pull the sheet over yourself."

But I don't. I just lie there looking at her picture on the wall and feeling the warm strip of sun across the chest. "When I was a kid I saw this model in a hobby shop and it cost twenty-five or thirty bucks, I forget exactly, and I *had* to have it. It was one of those things, you know, that people get hung up on. Like all teen-agers want a motorcycle, or something, and for me it was this model that I couldn't afford and that I knew I probably couldn't build even if I had it. My old man wouldn't even hear about it. He said it was another stupid whim that would last about three days. So I stole most of the money for it from him."

"Did it?"

"Did it what?"

"Did it last three days?"

"Yes . . . no. I mean it lasted a lot longer than that. I worked on it forever, it seems like."

From my shirt pocket on the chair by the bed I fish a cigarette and a book of matches. Light up and use my shoe for an ashtray.

"And?"

"And what?"

"And so what happened to it?"

"I don't know. I never finished it. It's probably still in my mother's attic in Santa Cruz. I took it with me when we moved from Santa Barbara."

Ellen lies back down and rests her head on my chest. I blow smoke in her hair and notice that my armpits are none too fragrant.

"Ryan?"

"What?"

"Will you get out of here, please. I'm beginning to feel rotten, however odd that may seem to you. How am I going to face Milt?" After the fact she's worried. Funny how the roles reverse. I don't feel a thing. Her voice seems distant, as if it is coming from another room.

Deep drag on my cigarette. "You know something," I say. "I'm going to go down and get that damn thing out of the attic and finish it."

She sits up suddenly and puts her hand over my mouth and I swallow a stomachful of smoke. "You lousy bastard.

You never listen to anything but the sound of your own voice. Come on, Ryan. Get up and hit the road. The show's over."

But the show isn't over. I grind my cigarette out in my shoe and reach over and crab-walk my fingers around her belly, up the valley between her breasts to her neck, and around one earlobe. After a bit she closes her eyes, shivers, and reaches for me. The second act is just beginning.

In the living room the telephone rings and with a groan Ellen swings her legs over the bed, picking her robe off the chair as she moves toward the door.

"Forget the phone and come back here."

She pauses in the doorway and throws me a half-angry grimace. "I'm going to kill Milt for not showing up last night. Will you please get dressed and get the hell out of here now." And she goes through the hall toward the phone. I look at my watch and see that it is almost eleven o'clock.

Reluctantly I roll off the warm bed with its stripe of sunlight and hunt my swimming suit in a jumbled pile of clothes by the dresser, and I'm standing in my bare ass with the trunks in my hand, humming a few bars of "Now's the Time" when I sense that she is back in the doorway. I look and her face seems the color of her sun-bleached hair and when she speaks her voice sounds as though she is under water. "They found Milt in a canyon near Pigeon Point."

When I move across the room toward her she shrinks back, hugging herself, and looks wild-eyed at me as if one of us is mad. She takes a few unsteady steps and crawls into the bed like a sick dog.

VI

π Far up above the barrier of pines great storm clouds are beginning to pile up, swirling mountains of gray-black over the granite walls of the Sierra, rain-streaked and shot with corridors of light. A shaft of sun finds its way through the maze, down the funnel of an air draft, and into my room on the second floor. Miraculous. Relentless. It falls across the desk, the typewriter, over the floor to the bed, and sits on my eyelids until I give up and open them.

A somber procession winds through the vaulted arch of an old stone church. Ancient walls of hand-hewn rock grown mossy in the damp of a thousand fogs, stained black at the lower heights by sap from the oleander shrubs that grow around their perimeter. A minister leads the way and he reads aloud from the order for the burial of the dead as he goes. "I am the resurrection and the life, saith the Lord: he that believeth in me, though he were dead, yet shall he live: and whosoever liveth and believeth in me, shall never die."

Behind the minister comes the stricken family. Mother weeping under her veil, holding a pale blue handkerchief over her nose and mouth. Anguished and miserable father holding himself stiff as a plank. He looks neither to the right nor to the left lest the sad eye of a friend crack through the shaky wall he has constructed for the occasion.

Milton's brother follows behind the mother and father. Too young to know what is going on. Bewildered and frightened by grief, not by death. He walks between Ellen and Ryan and they hold his hands. God knows what is in *their* heads; their faces are averted. Is that pity I see? Revulsion? Disgust? Horror? I can't say. Perhaps they will reveal themselves.

"I know that my redeemer liveth, and that he shall stand at the latter day upon the earth: and though this body be destroyed, yet shall I see God: whom I shall see for myself, and mine eyes shall behold, and not as a stranger." The minister reaches the altar and takes his place beside the coffin as his followers scatter out into the pews. Behind the coughs and rustles the organist plays Bach. "We brought nothing into this world, and it is certain we can carry nothing out. The LORD gave, and thee LORD hath taken away; blessed be the name of the LORD."

In the church a shaft of light streams through the stained glass over the altar. Christ hangs there in his opaque trap like a fly caught in amber. He looks sadly down at the coffin as the Twenty-seventh Psalm is being read, dims, brightens, winks on and off as the clouds scud across the sky. A neon savior. I see dust swirls in the shaft. Sequins on the sun. Lilies on the altar, and gladiolas. A wreath of white roses and carnations set back on an artist's easel behind the box. Everywhere flowers. Spring garden show at the Masonic temple. A corsage for death. Air like a junior prom. The organist is playing a selection from *Lohengrin* and a blackface minstrel does a soft shoe on the stage. The audience stands to watch the show. Clap your hands. *"In time of trouble* /clap/ *He shall hide me* /clap/ *In dat rock* /yea/ *In dat rock* /yea, yea/ *Oh, in de secret place* /yea, yea/ *Of his dwelling* /clap, clap/ *He shall hide me* /Oh Lord/ *In a rock of stone* /yea, men/."

Ellen stands in the pew wearing a white dress made of spun glass. With a broad, heavy-buckled belt she whips herself across the back saying, "One for you and one for me and one for you and one for me." She pays no attention to the music, and the congregation does not seem to notice her or hear her wail. I step over beside her and tell her to get with it, she's missing the beat, but she just stares at me with hollow eyes and then pulls her lips back over her teeth and snarls, "We must pay." She continues to swing the buckle. "One for you and one for me, one for you and one for me."

Up on the altar the blackface is beginning his address to the flowers. "Dearly beloved, we are gathered together here in the sight of God, and in the face of this company, to join together this Man and this Woman in holy matrimony; which is an honorable estate, instituted . . ." But I step out into the aisle and interrupt him. "Hey man. You've got the wrong scene here. This is a funeral, not a wedding."

"I believe not," he says.

"Believe not? There must be some mistake. Somebody is confused."

"No, man. No mistakes. No confusions. This here's the temple of holy happenings. This where you pay."

"Pay? For what do I pay?"

"Why, man, for the way you did your buddy while he was lying in the creek all messed up and sore."

Ellen comes up the aisle dressed in white spun glass and stands quietly by my side. "You made this chick feel guilty," he goes on. "And so you see, man, now you got to pay. You are the re*dee*mer. You are her salvation. You took up where your buddy left off. You wanted his chick and you got her. Now, you got to accept that. That's the rules. Ain't no cop-outs here."

"I didn't want her. I just . . ."

"Ah, but now you got her, man, and she feeling bad because of you and you got to put it right. Like, it's a question of responsibility. Somebody got to pay the piper. He don't play no gratis gigs."

"I'm not responsible for Mole's accident."

"No, man, but you responsible for a couple other accidents."

"Like what?"

"Like the crackup of her soul and for the future soul you created. You responsible for that."

"You're insane. Lunatic. What about souls? Creation of what soul?"

"Ah, dad, for the soul of the little cannon that explodes in the night. For the soul of the wriggly scriggly that goes forth like a hero into the dragon's lair. For the soul of the little tadpole that saved Humpty-Dumpty from a great fall. In short, my man, for the soul of the kiddy that is currently in the can. While your buddy was being knocked down his chick was being knocked up."

"Well, it's no deal. I'm not the only one who's been there."

"True. True. But since the other possibility has . . . ah . . . how shall I say it . . . been absolved of his mortality, that leaves us with you." Ellen's hand is on my arm and Blackface begins again to address the congregation. The sun is in my eyes and the roar of surf in my head.

"As I was saying, dearly beloved, we are gathered here to join this plaintiff and this defendant in holy matrimony. Most merciful Father, who hast been pleased to take unto thyself the soul of this servant; grant to us who are still in our pilgrimage, and who walk as yet by faith, that having served thee with constancy on earth, we may be joined in holy matrimony, or something like that. The LORD giveth and the LORD taketh away."

"So, into this holy estate these two sinners present come now to be joined. If any man can show just cause why they may not lawfully be joined together, let him now speak, or else keep his mouth shut in the hereafter, and so forth."

"I'll show you just cause," I cry. "This is an absurd joke. A union born not of love but of guilt and fear and repulsion."

"I am a necrophiliac," Ellen cries, laying about herself with the belt. "One for you and one for me and one for you . . ."

I turn to the minister. "You see? She's just trying to wipe out her sense of sin by getting married to it. This ceremony is an atrocity."

"A life for a life," intones the blackface, swinging a little pot of incense.

"I didn't take any life."

"No, dad. You made one."

"You don't *know* that."

"If you don't mind we'll continue."

"Man, that is born of a woman, hath but a short time to live, and is full of misery. He cometh up, and is cut down, like a flower; he fleeth as it were a shadow, and never continueth in one stay." Sound of weeping in the background. Father sits rigid in his seat.

"But be all that as it may. Wilt thou have this woman to thy wedded wife, to live together after God's ordinance in the holy estate of Matrimony?"

"Does it matter?"

"No. And wilt thou have this man to thy wedded husband? Wilt thou love him, comfort him, honor, and keep him in sickness?"

"I will keep him in sickness."

"Then unto Almighty God we commend the soul of our brother departed, and we commit his body to the ground; earth to earth, ashes to ashes, dust to dust; in sure and certain hope of the resurrection unto eternal life, through our Lord Jesus Christ. And so with this ring I thee wed: In the name of the Father, and of the Son, and of the Holy Ghost."

The minister raises his hands and I perceive that we are no longer in the church. The altar on which he had been standing is a cliff high up over the ocean and the congregation has disappeared. Ellen and I are hand in hand listening to a voice in the air. "O Almighty God, Creator of mankind, who only art the wellspring of life; bestow upon these thy servants, if it be thy will, the gift and heritage of children; and grant that they may see their children brought up in faith and fear. . . ."

In the distance I see a lodge and a group of cabins set out near the end of a headland and nearer, an old oak tree with a rubber tire swing hanging from one of its branches. Ellen and I stand at the edge of our field peering down at the rocks and spray a thousand feet below as a coffin gently disappears beneath the kelp-strewn waves. Behind us there is only a sea of poppies and the voice in the air.

"O merciful Father, whose face the angels of thy little ones do always behold in heaven; Grant us steadfastly to believe that this thy child hath been taken into the safe keeping of thine eternal love."

The voice stops, leaving us to the crash of the surf and the cry of gulls as they soar below us over the rocks. And suddenly Ellen is gone, and the field and the sea. The shaft of sunlight across my desk and typewriter has faded and the storm blowing down from the peaks has swallowed up the sky. With the first clap of thunder over the hospital the rain begins to streak the panes on my window. I shut my eyes and close up the carnival for the night.

VII

π Over the hills of the past hazy dreams march like Childe Roland to the dark tower. Through thistles and cactus and the dead leaves of eucalyptus they follow a crooked path and meet themselves both going and coming. The Lord gives and takes away and gives again in visions and revisions.

In a house on the eastern side of the coast range mountains, just below the summit, we wait for birth—or rebirth. I ask her to forget the past. Or is it she who asks me? We live in the shadow of an unspoken guilt, but what more can I do? I made her my wife. We should share and share alike. But she denies her guilt and says it is only mine: says it is only in my head. We drop the subject. In our bedroom on the mountain we make believe and call it love.

The house is built on the steep side of a canyon and is propped up in front by a row of telephone-pole pilings. There is a porch built out over nothing and it is held by a second row of poles. From below it looks like the underside of a pier or bridge and you can see the sky through the cracks in the planking.

In the mornings I stand on the porch clearing my sinus and spitting fifty feet down into the tangled brush that chokes the ravine. Winter dawns are best. The cloud cover is all down below, blanketing the peninsula for fifty miles, and the air on the mountain is as clear and brittle as glass. The sun begins to climb out of the rolling hills across the bay and a rose-gray tide of fire washes across the valley, glows hot red, still hotter orange, white-hot gold. The clouds melt away and I see the fifty-mile housing tract that stretches from San Francisco to San Jose, squatting in the smog of its own excrement.

Except in the dryest part of the summer a stream runs down the canyon, splashing its way over the rocks and burbling beneath a tangle of fallen trees and brush. I lie in bed at night listening to it sing with the tree frogs and crickets. I smell again the earthy vapor of bay and Scotch broom and leaf mold that floats around the house and mingles with the faintly sour odor of wet redwood shingles.

Behind the house there is a broad, grassy bench, protected from the summer sun by towering redwood trees whose branches jut over the clearing and over part of the house. On foggy evenings their dripping sounds like rain on the roof . . . sounds like dreary nights out of the past . . . eucalyptus and seed pods. Visions and revisions. Pictures at an exhibition.

On a sunny morning after a damp night of fog Ellen sits on the deck in a bat-winged chair. I remember I brought coffee out from the kitchen and I spilled some of it on the already wet wood. The planks steam in the sun. She sits with the cup in her lap and watches a hawk circle below us in the canyon, his wings never moving as he glides on the drafts and currents that sweep over the hills. "I'd give anything," she says, "to be able to float around like that; to fly over the mountains like a dream and never have to move a muscle or touch my feet down on the earth. Watch all the people scurrying down below. I'd just drift on the air and never come down."

"Yeah? I bet Mole would have given anything to be able to do that too."

Ellen stops watching the hawk and studies her lap instead. She looks less dreamy. "I'd give anything," she says, "if you'd stop bringing that up day after day." She gets heavily out of the chair and goes inside.

The house has two levels but the rooms down below are dark and moldy. Their backs are dug into the earth and their fronts overhung by the porch. The windows look out into a double row of pilings, most of them rotten at the base, and only two of the six poles that hold up the deck are functional. I make my study in one of the rooms and when I am not at the university I spend most of my time there. A fitting place to pursue the study of English literature. Grendel's lair all cruddy and foul. To be a scholar you must be a troglodyte and pass the monotony of consciousness in soggy holes.

Ellen goes into my cave only once and without my knowledge or permission. I come home from school, where I have been delivering myself of a seminar paper, and find her locked in the bedroom. She will not open the door or answer me when I call to her, and then I hear her sobbing. "Leave me alone." Hysterics. Theatrics. "Ghoul."

I understand where she has been and I rush down to my crypt to see if she has destroyed the shrine over my bookcase. She has, but it lies on the daybed, its brim still pinned on one side, and the no-longer-yellow garter still around its crown.

We sit in the house on the mountain and wait for birth: Ellen in a chair under the window, looking as if she has swallowed a whale, and Ryan stretched out on the couch. In the center of the picture, directly between the chair and the couch, I see a massive stone fireplace with its mouth full of ashes and cigarette butts. The window emits very little light and the room is filled with vague forms and shadows.

Ryan talks and I watch. Always I watch. I see Ellen's belly grow larger by the day. Saw the tadpole become a frog, become a fish, become a whale. It floats in a dark and quiet ocean and waits for the world to be born.

"What shall we name him?" she asks.

"How about Jonah?"

"Very funny. Be serious, love."

"Okay. How about Milton?"

Ellen keeps her eyes on her knitting and the room is very quiet. "Please. You promised no more."

"I'll settle for Jonah, then."

She continues knitting and her needles click in the dusky room. A cat wanders in from the kitchen and sits on the cold hearth, licking the bottom of one paw. He stops, puts the paw down, and begins to circle around on the bricks, dragging his bottom. Wormy grin on his face.

"Why can't we stop bringing Milton up all the time?" Ellen says. "Why can't we just forget and start making a life for ourselves and our baby?"

"*Our* baby?"

Ellen picks up her knitting and walks into the bedroom. She closes the door behind her and Ryan grins back at the cat.

At one corner of the flat clearing behind the house there is a huge metal sculpture, cut and shaped and welded from various parts of wrecked cars. Its creator is Gunboat Larson, now living in a woods-secluded cabin several miles south along the ridge of the coast range mountains. Ryan assists him and together they build the monster in less than a month.

The figure is fourteen feet high and they call it Modern Man. Its head is no larger than a softball and is absurdly distorted on top of the massive shoulders. Its painted eyes are without pupils and its mouth is a jagged hole cut with the torch. Modern Man pushes a wheelbarrow in which his enormous testicles are riding. The testicles are covered with gunnysacking and are ten times the size of his head, and from the bend in his knees Modern appears to strain under his load. If Ellen looked closely she might recognize the door panels of her old MG forming the upper portion of his back.

Ellen sits in the chair under the window and folds her hands over her stomach. There is no knitting and no cat in the picture; only the fireplace with its dead ashes. I can hear the whale breathing, spouting, down in the liquid center of mother earth, and in the belly of the whale a tortured life stomps and raves to be set free. *The waters compassed me about, even to the soul: the depth closed me round about, the weeds were wrapped about my head.* Poppy suns in front of my eyes and an orange ball floating with the kelp heads. Light. Oppressive light all around me and Ryan's voice droning in the top of my skull. "The time is close. He must have a name . . . a name."

"It may be a girl."

"No."

"Call him what you like."

Can the time be so close? Eight months. Nine. Nine months since the funeral? Or was it a wedding? How long for a whale to get born? Time is like a roar in my ears; like a steam engine running late along a winding mountain track. Will it never, *ever,* catch up?

The Lord speaks to Ellen and Ellen speaks to the whale. It vomits up Jonah upon the dry land, and we look at his red, helpless body and change his name to Ryan. In the corridor of the hospital I peer through the glass window into a toothless pink howl. Dr. Somebody shakes my hand. "Fine boy."

"How come he yells like that?"

"Well, he's probably frightened and uncomfortable. Where he's been it's warm and dark and quiet. Liquid and soft. Nothing to do but sleep. All of a sudden he's jerked out into the light. Strange smells, strange noises. Smacked on the bottom, washed, wrapped in a diaper, and put in a room with a lot of other yowlers."

"Nothing much ever changes does it?"

"Beg pardon?"

Five months after the baby is born the front porch falls off the house. Prophetic. Life runs along a track as unswerving as a merry-go-round.

"How many of the little brass rings did you get, Ryan?"

"Not a one."

PART FOUR

I

π There will be a terrible storm over our part of the mountains. I watched it build over the peaks as I sat at my writing desk and I could see tongues of lightning flicker in the darkest mass of clouds to the northeast. It moved imperceptibly and after a bit I gave up waiting for it and opened a large package sent to me by an old friend in San Francisco. The box once contained White Horse Scotch and I am saving it because it reminds me of a tavern in New York where I once drank eleven boilermakers before I fell off the stool and was taken to a flophouse on lower Third Avenue by a kindly cabby in whose hack I puked.

The package has nothing of much interest in it. Some books I left here and there—a complete set of Mark Twain, a paperbacked copy of *The Floating Opera,* a Gideon Bible, a collection of Elizabethan plays, two copies of *Seven Keys to Baldpate,* which I'm glad to have because it gives my present residence a certain perspective. There are some old letters and a diary that I never kept with any regularity or enthusiasm. Scattered fragments of the past that tell a hundred tedious stories if the right interpreter is available—somebody with enough imagination to give flair and color to a drab history of defection.

There are old term papers—three that I wrote myself, one that I copied from Charles Mason's undergraduate thesis done at Yale. No chance of getting caught there, hey Charlie? Lousy paper, though, my friend. Dull. Very much like you. I can scarcely believe I had the courage to present your nincompoopery to a contemporary literature seminar.

IMPRESSIONISM

Philosophical Impressionism, an outgrowth of empiricism and the romantic movement, establishes reality entirely in the stream of sensations. Fundamentally, impressionism is a statement of the subjectivity of reality and the variety of individual responses to collective experience.

Oh, Charlie. What an ass you are. What a tedious pedant. I can hear laughter in the dark right now.

Memory, imagination, and emotion guide the mind in its ordering of individual consciousness and become the basis for artistic representation of experience.

And I am reading this drivel to people who are supposed to think. I am having some trouble locating myself in this room. My mind is a vulture that keeps picking open the bars at the back of my skull and flapping around the room listening to me drone on and on, listening to the speaker drone on and on, listening to other voices in other rooms drone on and on. . . .

Reality, insofar as it is definable, is primarily the images and impressions in the mind.

Then this is real. I am disjointed. I am unhinged. I have at last achieved an impression of *myself*. The casing has cracked and I am peering into the septic tank of my soul. Black narcissus. There is nothing there to love. I see the miserable skeleton of a whining, cheating, lying sinner whose translucent flesh hangs foul on its props, legs besmeared with excrement, breath reeking like dead fish, eyes yellow and sick as a bloody egg.

As Arnold Hauser has said, the impressionist's world, "the phenomena of which are in a state of constant flux and transition, produces the impression of a continuum in which everything coalesces, and in which there are no other differences but the various approaches and points of view of the beholder."

Everything coalesces in a dark, dank wood through which a narrow path runs between the crowded trees. I am laboring along that path; hemmed in, oppressed, weary. The woods grow darker and danker and the path more overgrown. My wretchedness increases as I struggle along until even Job would think his afflictions minor by comparison. There is no place to go but on, winding around the woods. Spotted beasts slip through the trees and a wolf howls from a ravine. The skeleton dances on ahead of me, now slinking like a cur, now bumping and grinding like a belly dancer. I cry after it to stop. I can't go on. My anguish is so extreme that I must lie down on the path and die. But it dances on, beckoning, and I am forced to follow.

In the heart of the forest the path splits and the fork we follow ascends a hill. My breath comes in rasps, my heart pumps like a bellows, I am dizzy and sick and when we come to a spring that courses out of the rocks I faint away with exhaustion. A voice drones in my head. . . .

> The idea of associational thinking and the emphasis on the imagination, on the internal, as the primary reality are essentially philosophic aspects of impressionism.

Can the fool still be talking to his classmates? I have a brief vision, a dream, of a polished oak seminar table around which young men and women are sitting. There are fluorescent lights in the ceiling and a vulture, perched on the back of a chair, croaks out its message to the group.

> . . . at all costs to reveal the flickering of that innermost flame which flashes its message through the brain . . .

There is a heavy peal of thunder. A storm is approaching the mountains through which we wander. Tongues of lightning flicker in the rolling clouds to the northeast and I can see ahead of me, when the flashes illuminate the valley, the entrance to a pit around which white devils are dancing with black gnomes. They are dancing out of the pit and into the sky where they form a solid wall of symmetrically interlocked figures. In the center stands my skeleton-soul, beckoning, and I must come.

There is a circular chute like a children's slide at a playground that disappears into the blackness of the hole, and down it we travel, whirling around and around, past a howling Charon, past the suspended, past Minos and Cerberus. Down and down. Never stopping. The hoarders, the spendthrifts, the wrathful. Through the gates of Dis and across the burning sands. Down and down. Past the panderers and seducers, the flatterers, hypocrites, thieves, frauds, liars, until at last my guide stands with chattering grin pointing to a passageway at the bottom of the chute. When I run and look I see that the white devils and black gnomes have solidified in its core, like concrete, and the passage is blocked up forever.

While some knowledge is possible, and while we can get closer and closer to truth by examining a subject from a variety of angles and depths, we can never know everything about that subject, and our judgments, moral and otherwise, will always be based ultimately on subjective impressions. Thank you very much, and if you have any questions I'll be happy to try and answer them.

I have two questions, please. First, why did you copy that incredibly foolish paper, and second, is it really true that I am going mad? Or would you say that I've always *been* mad?

The wind begins to whip the trees around, bending their tips and blowing twigs and cones all over the lawn. I can hear the thunder much closer as the clouds roll leaden and gray down from the peaks. No rain yet, but the lightning pops in the heavy overcast and lights the sky like a flashbulb in a darkened theater. We are in for a blast up here at our retreat . . . home away from home . . . treasure of the Sierra Nevada. King Lear will start to rage in his padded cell, beating at his gate, letting folly in and judgment out. Rage, King. Crack your cheeks. Play hell with the fool orderlies. Make them work for their buck and a quarter an hour. We'll have cataracts and hurricanes. Thunderbolts that will rattle the very teeth of the mountains. Give it all you've got, nuncle. Tear the stuffing off the wall. The earth may indeed blow into the sea and bury once and for all the restless bones of sons and daughters.

There is a five-by-eight photograph of Ellen taken in the woods at Point Reyes during one of our trips up there. Taken by Michael, I think, though I can't remember the occasion or when he sent us the print. Strange how after staring at a picture for a while you can't remember how the person really looks. Ten minutes ago I could see Ellen in my head and now all I see is a five-by-eight gloss print. The boy I can remember in every detail: the thin arms with a suntan line where the sleeve of his T-shirt came down, the texture of his hair and the two cowlicks just above his collar, the tiny mole behind his earlobe, the scar on his kneecap from a fall on concrete. And the way he walked and ran and talked and cried and ate and slept. . . . I can remember all that. I see it. I have no photograph. I see fields of poppy and a rocky coast in the background. Spray exploding off the stacks and kelp bobbing in the swells. And I hear the blues playing through the radio of an overturned sport car.

> I'm tired of marryin', tired of this settlin' down;
> Tired of bein' married, tired of this settlin' down—
>   Shuckin' Sugar—
> I want to stay like I am, slip from town to town.

I have her photograph but I can't recall her face. Good title for a popular song. I have no recording but I sure can hear her sing. "What's the matter? Are you ill? Why don't you buckle down to work? How long are we going to live in this hovel on my part-time job and what we can sponge off my mother? Why don't you finish this damn degree so that we can live like human beings? Get a carrel in the stacks and work there between classes. I can't stand having you hang around the house all day. God. I wish I'd married a salesman."

Then a month or two of worry. "Ryan, please. See a doctor. You act funny all the time. Is it me? . . . something I'm doing that bugs you? . . . some way I act or look? We haven't made love in almost a month, you know? Tell me what's wrong . . . or if you can't tell me see a doctor and tell him. Can't we work it out? If I didn't love you so much I wouldn't care . . . I wouldn't worry . . . but I can't stand this never-ending silence."

Silence is what I need. Absolute quiet. No questions, answers, problem-solving discussions. No dealings. No feelings. Let us not spread our guts on the table and paw through them, searching for cancers to eradicate, tumors to snip, messy collections of fat to clean up, veins and arteries to polish. Let us be quiet. Let us not have conversation because conversation leads to relationship and relationship leads to involvement and involvement leads to questions and answers and problem-solving discussions. I don't want my problems solved. I want them dissolved. And for that I need quiet. Absolute silence in which to suspend my mind. I need to concentrate on not thinking, on keeping every little vagrant thought barred from the threshold of consciousness, on erasing every tiny vision and revision from the map of my brain. Only then can I escape this intruder who oversees my every act. I feel like a bit player doing triple, quadruple service in a single play; being walked through my parts by a relentless director, changing my clothes, my masks. "Get the scene, Ryan? You're the understudy so we want you to take the falls during rehearsals. No use in banging up the star for an empty house. Mole is going to come on and speak the lines but you take the tumble."

I need to be alone. I need some dark, quiet hole in a remote wombing house. Even my puns nauseate me. I need to sit in liquid quiet like a defunct fetus in its jar of formaldehyde; placed away on a dusty shelf where nothing but the crack of doom will disturb me. When the call to judgment blows I will run to the bosom of my maker and plead temporary insanity.

The wind stopped—very suddenly—and the trees quit blowing and everything is dead still, as if nature has sucked in her breath and is seeing how long she can hold it before the seven soundings of the trumpets. From the window I can see the thunderheads piled a thousand feet above, black on blacker black, like great slouching beasts come to make war on the mountain.

There is a blue book with the university seal on the front and lines for name, date, and course number. It bears my signature and underneath: "Latin Examination, in partial fulfillment of the requirements for the degree of Doctor of Philosophy."

> Son of Anchises, born of godly line,
> By night, by day, the portals of dark Dis
> Stand open: it is easy, the descending
> Down to Avernus. But to climb again,
> To mark the footsteps back to the air above,
> There lies the task, the toil. . . .

Translation, as I recall, by an undergraduate classics major behind the locked doors of an empty office while I sat twiddling a pencil, never looking at the passage. Ironic. I knew it by heart, and still do. "A few, beloved by Jupiter, descending from the gods, a few, in whom exalting virtue burned, have been permitted. Around the central woods in black Cocytus glides, a sullen river; but if such love is in your heart, such longing for double crossing of the Stygian lake, for double sight of Tartarus, learn first what must be done. In a dark tree there hides a bough, all golden, leaf and pliant stem, sacred to Proserpine."

Ah Lord, I follow my skeleton into distant visions. Back along the path that runs through grief and fear and spectral horror. I follow a polluted stream into nether hell. Where is my Acneas to raise a sword in my defense? Where is my Virgil to guide me through the maze and out once more to look upon the stars? I hear the lamentations of children's souls at the gates of hell and I know my boy is among them. Oh pardon, Minos, pardon. Release me from torment. Slay the vulture whose neck is bloody with my liver gore.

What is it the divine priestess had said? "Their crimes were not to have loved a brother while love was allowed them." And something about having inveigled a dependent. No matter. Enough of these excursions. Ellen is right —was right. Books are bad for me. I take them to heart, absorb them, confuse them with reality. Perhaps they brought on the return of my separation. It grew day by day, week by week, more and more continual until I felt like a double shadow walking around the university in a vague dream, being pushed this way and that with no will of my own to revolt.

II

π There is an old letter in my box from the Dean of Graduate Studies at the university saying, "To whom it may concern. The qualifying examination for the degree of Doctor of Philosophy will be held on August 15 through 19 from eight to twelve A.M."

The department chairman said, "Apply yourself diligently, my boy, and you should have no difficulty. I can remember myself, a hundred and thirty years ago, faced with the same terrifying doubts about my ability to confront the moment and push it to its crisis (a footnote to Mr. Eliot there, heh), but one must take a firm grip and realize the comprehensive examination we all have faced is but a rite of passage into a lifetime of intellectual struggle . . . the point has slipped me. No matter. There is still much time for study. Get to it."

Ryan said, "You'll never make it. In six weeks you can't prepare for twenty hours of testing. Think, you ass. The whole of English and American literature and you have to know something about all of it. And if you take it and fail? How will you look then? How will you look your fellows in the eye and tell them you don't give a damn: that you only took the test on the half chance that you might slide by but that you didn't much expect to since you only put in half a week of study during the whole summer while they were laboring eight, ten, twelve hours a day over their books. What excuse will you give that will ring true? What excuse will you believe? And how will you avoid their mock pity, their 'Gee, that's rough' and the whispered conversations around the department, 'Everyone but Ryan.' Forget it, man, or start building a defense."

Ryan and Ellen argued. She said, "Rye, you can do it! You have six weeks and you're not exactly starting from scratch. All you have to do is review and you'll get through easily. Please try. *Please*. I can't stand it if you drag it out another year. Don't go to the ball game this afternoon. The Giants will survive without you. Just start working."

We went to the ball game and the Giants lost one to nothing. Mays whiffed twice and Davenport was beaned by a wild pitch.

Endless arguments with Ellen. "It's not just a matter of reviewing stuff I already know, it's learning a whole lot I don't. Like I've never even *had* a course in Shakespeare. I haven't read more than three plays in my whole life. I know nothing about Restoration comedy. Not even the name of a single playwright. I'm not sure when the Restoration even *was*. You don't just gloss over those gaps in six weeks while you're reviewing the history of world lit from Beowulf to Bowles. I can't do it this time around."

Ellen said, "You've got to do it. My mother isn't going to go on coughing up two hundred bucks a month for-ever, and we sure can't live off my part-time job at the press. Anyway, I'd think your self-respect would begin to bug you."

III

π From up on the ridge there is a tremendous clap of thunder that rattles the building like the quake that felled Babylon and the calm is shattered. The trees begin to thrash once again and pebbles of rain ricochet off the window. The caves begin to run sheets of water and the afternoon is turned into night. Switch on my lamp and continue reading. Ignore the wrath of God and his judgment voices. Believe in the New Jerusalem for I shall build it with my own two hands. Everyman an Alpha and Omega, say I.

In my bundle there is a cursory note from the department chairman asking me to explain my absence from the qualifying examinations given on August 15 through 19. Why did I keep that, I wonder? It begins, "It is regrettable that you were unable to find within yourself the strength to confront a crisis that we must all, as scholars and aspiring teachers, eventually face. One can only evade so long . . ." and it ends on the same minor key.

Water is seeping under my windowsill. Damn the rain. It will be too sodden tomorrow to walk in the garden.

He took me to San Francisco because he had an appointment there with another medievalist and I was late getting to his office. We drove up the Bayshore Freeway and he explained for thirty-five miles why I had not "faced up" and I stared out the window at the billboards. I remember the Redwood City Tannery; abandoned, faded red buildings set out in a field of filthy rubble, spears of marsh grass and coyote brush, yellow adobe soil baked and cracked in which the semicircles of discarded tires poked up like croquet wickets. How could I tell him that my problem was not the one he imagined at all? How could I say, "The reason I didn't show is because I was in prison, because I am now in prison, because I always will *be* in prison unless I pick the lock and vanish"? How could I say, "I don't want in. I want out"? How could I tell him that Mole and Ellen and Michael and Stevenson and my poor old, single-winged father (yes, and even the boy) have got me under a bell glass and are making me hop like a cricket against the invisible dome they have constructed? Would he understand me if I said "the more you know, the more you grow, the more you *owe*"?

I DON'T OWE ANYBODY ANYTHING.

Somewhere around Burlingame (I remember the fog was spilling down through a notch in the hills and drifting across the bay) he leaned sideways and unconsciously farted. He lowered the window automatically, as if by habit, and I began to pity the seat cushion. I began to think how a seat cushion's life is like a man's life and then I began to imagine that I *was* a seat cushion and I had just absorbed a fart on the back of my neck that was dispersing through the fibers of my body—poisoning me, putrefying my flesh, turning my veins into sewer pipes. I was nauseated and dizzy and I thought I was going to have to ask him to stop and let me out, but the spell passed away. Then I began to feel sorry for *him* because it seemed as if the making of a fleeting smell was the only means he had to indicate that he existed. He had become metamorphosed into the books he read and the books he wrote and the rattle in his anus was like a tiny cry in the wilderness, "I'm still here, I'm still here." Medieval dialects seemed so irrelevant, so remote and useless and dead, that I wanted to turn to him and beg him to come back into the world: to say "Mr. Ormulum, there are people who dig ditches, and sail boats, and pave roads, and cut trees, and teach skiing, and build houses, and report news, and drive trucks, and salvage junk, and their farts and belches and sweats are come by honestly and are passed into the atmosphere by the winds that blow around their heads. But yours are all absorbed by the pad on your desk chair where they are cooped up forever, locked in a prison of foam rubber and plastic, and when you die they will put that pad on the shelf with your musty old books and say here are the collected gases of Ormulus Ormulum, verbal and excremental: he was a ripe scholar and exceedingly wise, but nobody cared." When he let me out on Polk Street in the fog he asked me to come to the post-exam party.

A lightning bolt splits a tree in the corner of the park and knocks its top clear out onto the lawn. The blast is so tremendous that it might have been a bomb or dynamite exploding and there is a smell of ozone throughout the building. I expect some of the patients are convinced we have come to the end of time—particularly the prophet in Ward 3 who quotes to me from Revelations as we walk in the garden. I wish I had a white horse. I'd ride it up and down the corridor and call his name. I'd say, "Hey there, Jonathan Divine, come on out, John boy. Fear not. I'm the first and the last. I'm he that lives and was dead; and behold, I'm for ever, Amen; and I have the keys of hell and of death right here in my pocket, Amen." John would wet his pants with joy and they'd cart him off for more shock treatments.

There is also a carbon copy of a letter I wrote to Ormulum asking him to forgive me for spoiling his party. Where the original went I haven't any idea, but I'm quite sure I never sent it. Amazing how one can weave a narrative out of scraps of paper if one selects properly. There is much I leave out. Letters from my mother, from Ellen, from the draft board; some poems and half a short story. Perhaps I'll find a use for them another time. I could use a white seedless grape now but there is none in my box so I'll have to pretend.

Orm's party was a lugubrious affair and I should not have gone. Ellen refused. She said we had no business there since I had not taken the exams, but something drew me even though I was uneasy. I sat in my old Ford for quite a long time before I went in. How was it exactly? I've forgotten. Smoking cigarettes and debating whether to flee or stay? Can't remember anymore. I could use some pictures now. Print up some pictures, please, and write a story to go with them. The rain blowing against the window sounds like sand.

Ryan slumps behind the wheel of his parked car. Takes out another cigarette and pushes in the lighter. (You need the key on, stupid.) Chill in the air, though the day has been warm. Goose-bump night like all California nights. No James Agee twilights with shirt sleeves and fireflies and the sound of hoses sprinkling the lawns. A woman in a fur coat comes down the street walking a nervous minia-ture poodle. He hops along as if the ground is hot; skitters from tree to tree; lifts his leg in salute at each one; destroys a row of juniper. The woman drags him on by.

Ryan gets out of the car and angles across the street to-ward the house. A foursome of latecomers precedes him up the walk, still talking about the exams.

"How did you like the Medieval questions?"

"Not bad. Least they weren't written in Old English. Ha Ha."

"Oh listen. I just clutched the first day. I just blanked out I tell you. I was so shook I wrote about Gawain and the jolly green giant. Ha ha ha ha."

(This is becoming tedious. Just get on with it, please. Get into the party. What happens?)

Ryan feels out of place and depressed and everything begins to seem artificial. People are having nylon thoughts and are speaking plastic words. Their clothes are all Orlon and Dacron. The flowers on the table are wax and a gas log burns in the fireplace. Everything is stiff and brittle and he keeps thinking that a loud noise, a sonic boom or something, could reduce the whole house and its congre-gation to a great pile of shattered synthetics. The only thing that is real is the Scotch and he starts to get drunk, hoping that it will make him feel normal again. After a while he goes to the bathroom and sees himself in the long mirror over the sink. Ridiculous grin. Face rigid as a plank from two hours of smiling at the gray-headed ladies who always corner the losers at a party. Jaws ache and he pulls at my face to get it mobile: labial cramp seems to extend up to the top of my skull and my cheeks keep springing back into the ridiculous grin. As he stares he suddenly becomes aware that I am being watched; that the reflection in the mirror is peering at me with a pleasant, placid smile. The flesh around the smile begins to recede, the teeth behind the red lips become more prominent, and their gleam is intense. "Go away," I whisper. The lips mimic but the voice seems to come from a distance as if someone else has spoken. Am I looking in or am I looking out? Is he the voice or the ears? The two are not connected. Perhaps some connection in my brain short-circuited one hot day on the beach. I listen for the muffled *fzzzz* of frayed wires making contact in my skull but hear only a knocking at the gate. "Someone in there?" I've got to get out of this mess —out of the bathroom, out of the party, out of the university, out of my life. I must go where no one can find me; to silence and darkness where there will be no distant voices to confuse me and no light to cast my shadow. "I say, is someone in there?"

In the barnyard the chickens are still crowing and Chaunticlere Ormulum struts around with a tray of martinis. On the living room table there is a bunch of real fruit in a green glass bowl and Ryan picks a seedless grape and goes into a corner to peel it. Sticks it in his nose, lower half hanging out on his lip.

He walks around the room with my grape. His hands are in my pockets and his eyes are on a star. It seems as if he is the moon and the others are the tides. He shines in the living room and they flow to the dining room. He casts pale beams in the den and they swell toward the kitchen. People keep drifting off like jellyfish in the surf. His fellow students are casting envious glances in my direction. Jealous sublunar creatures, they are wishing they had attained such ethereal heights. Orm's wife comes up and says, "I think you need a handkerchief," and thanking her, he reaches up with thumb and forefinger, squashes the grape all over my lip. She is caught by a passing wave and washed toward shore.

There is an end to this story. An afterword. An appendix full of watermelon seeds. Ryan tells Ellen about grapes and she tells him about foxes. She is not amused. She calls him down. Gets excited about "self-destruction." She starts to yell and then to cry and the boy, who is now almost three, wakes up and adds his anemic wail to the melodic line. Uncanny, the effect. Harmonics, dissonances, do-it-yourself Strindberg. It grates on my ears and yet secretly I am amused because it is all coming to a close. I have not had to pick the lock. The door was open all the time and only the opportunity that was lacking. Now let them fight: let the battle rage. At the peak of their fury, when hatred obliterates all thought, and reason bows to passion, when their craws are burning with venomous bile, and their shriekings are amplified by their desire to rip, tear, destroy—then will I tiptoe out the back door and, smiling into my hand, slip off where I shall never be found. I shall vanish with the night.

IV

π Over the freeway to paradise. Take the Northbeach off-ramp or you'll find yourself on the Bay Bridge to Oakland. Take the last exit. Last lap of the journey that is by no means free. Last alley of escape over which the maimed in spirit and crippled in mind, the junkies, drunks, and Jesus-seekers, the homeless and hopeless, the tea heads, acid heads, juice heads pour into Nirvana looking for the Zen Master who will show them the way out. There is no further place to run.

> *the sea, delaying not hurrying not, whisper'd me through the night, and very plainly before daybreak lisp'd to me the low and delicious word, death*

Oh, my Guru, where are you now?

In my journal I wrote: "In dilapidated Howard Street

hotels, dreary-bleary old men nod and dream and smoke the discarded butts of Montgomery Street affluence, until one day, with myopic unconcern, they drop the ash that transforms their collapsing throne of horsehair and stuffing into a belch of acrid smoke and greasy fire. In the Tenderloin a faded whore cuts her throat in the bathtub of her cheap rented room. Or maybe somebody cut if for her. Who cares? In the Mission district a middle aged woman spatters her mind like a Jackson Pollock painting on the cracked and peeling walls of her basement apartment and then sits down suddenly in a litter of empty gin bottles. In the enclosed garden of a fashionable Pacific Heights town house an exhausted debutante unties the silk sash from the French curtains in her second floor bedroom, knots it around her neck and the balcony railing, and steps off into roses. A fuddled father leaps from the Golden Gate Bridge with his baby in his arms and inaugurates Family Plan flights for the year. The mommies and daddies are coming. Like lemmings to the sea. Like pioneers in their covered wagons. Fords, Chevys, Lincolns, Cadillacs. Face east, back to where you have been, and fling over the rail like a piece of used Kleenex. Late baptism of salt water and kelp."

At least the rain has stopped, though the trees are still cut off midway by the heavy mist. I used to think despair was fashionable. Seek out a sordid surrounding and wallow in it. I saw too many underground movies. Realism on all fives.

I made my escape to a flat on the top floor of an old converted warehouse in the produce district. Huge brown shiplap structure with its windows painted black on the ground level and a faded yellow and red sign, B. MORELLI AND SONS, painted clear across the front of the building. Once a big-time egg dealer, now a corpse. His sons have moved to fruits and vegetables in new quarters farther south.

The front door, also black, leads into an immense single room that was once the storage space for millions of eggs waiting to be boxed and crated and sent out on trucks. The room is only slightly less black than the door and the windows. A path of raised slats leads to the end of the building where the stairs walk up to the second and third floor. Walk up thinking, *He will not find me here. No one will find me here.* Walk up and down, ten times a day, fifteen, thinking, *Here I am safe from the warped shadows that haunt my waking dreams. He will not find me here.* Pause on the second floor landing and look down the hall off which the one-time offices of B. Morelli and his sons open —empty now, save one which is occupied by a whiskery goon named Melvin Warhole from Cedar Rapids. Occupation: writer. Activities: hating Jews and the FBI and mooching drinks in the Coffee Gallery on Grant Avenue. Walk up to the third floor thinking, *No one will find me here.* Pause on the landing in front of an impossible mirror that squints down the hallway at my door on the end. A full length incongruity in a gilt frame. Night watchman, maître d', keeper of all the souls who have looked into its meretricious eye. Dark glass. Insatiable swallower of images. You cannot keep mine. I have left it behind me.

Halfway down the corridor their is a firebox on the wall. Inside, an axe for smashing things and a ribbon candy of hose with a tarnished brass nozzle dangling at the end. Some comedian has opened the case and cut the hose in half. The hallway ceiling has lost its plaster and the laths are showing.

My room is not the kind you find hi-fied and low-lighted on the pages of *Playboy*. No apple-bottomed broad draped across a zebra-skin couch. No frozen daiquiris waiting on a teak bar. No chrome and leather chairs and no bear rugs on the floor. At night the street is silent and poorly lighted and nobody walks there until four in the morning when the produce workers show up. Push open the window and you can almost hear the water lapping against the wharves two blocks away. In the room a couch converts into a bed, a low coffee table of some much-stained and scarred blond wood squats in front of it favoring a bandaged leg, an antiqued bureau grows stenciled flowers on its drawers. There is a metal table next to the sink in the corner, bare floors spattered with paint, and under the windows brick-and-board bookshelves with unloved paperbacks waiting for their spines to be broken. The previous tenant found a packing case full of egg cartons in the basement and with a staple gun he acousticized the ceiling. Unfortunate inspiration. The mice find the egg cups an excellent nesting place and their ramblings have made the bogus tile resemble a marble cake. Vaguely.

The room is large and on the front corner of the building so that it has windows facing two streets. During the day the produce trucks and stacks of crated vegetables clog the sidewalks and street. Across from my window there is always a mountain of boxes marked *GOLDEN RULE*. Do unto others before they do unto you. Do it with a grapefruit. Red net onion sacks bulging with pearly fruit are stacked to the top of a one-ton truck and all day long there are curses in Italian as the truckers load and unload.

There are several grounds keepers out on the lawn

checking the storm damage and apparently discussing what to do with the top of the pine tree knocked down by the lightning. A chain saw will disturb the peace and I doubt they want to cut it by hand.

When I remember that room it seems as if there is a fur wrapping around my head. A mink tea cozy in which everything is warm and quiet and dark. I was alone. My bugbear had vanished—ditched in Palo Alto or Woodside —and I neither knew nor cared what he was doing. It was only a short walk to the Simmons mattress factory where I worked. Now and then I worked, since the last to be hired is the first to be fired when things drop off. The noise from the Embarcadero would wake me in the morning and I'd fold up my bed and make myself breakfast on the hot plate. Make myself a cup of tepid tea from the hot water tap, make myself a fried egg and peanut butter sandwich for lunch, make myself sick with a pipe I tried to substitute for cigarettes. At seven-fifteen I'd go out into the cold morning with a paperback in my hip pocket (break its spine after lunch) and start to walk. Walk along the waterfront as the sun begins to warm the piers, and the freight trucks are already stacked up, loading, unloading; men loafing around the vans, talking, smoking the first cigar of the day while the fork lifts zip in and out of the docks like windup toys. Dead stop to full speed ahead. There is a mocha fudge smell in the air; coffee and choco-late from the Folger's and Ghiradelli plants near by. Walk down along the Embarcadero past Jack's Waterfront Hang-out and check the new ships in their berths. *Hawaiian Wholesaler* with the depth marking on her prow showing only a nine-foot draw. Empty. No action on her decks, which I can't see anyway because they are sixty feet above me and two years gone.

On the *William Luckenbach* seamen are over the side chipping paint, laying down a new coating of heavily leaded goop; shouting, spitting forty, fifty feet into the lime-colored water. Rainbows on the oil slick when a gob smacks the surface. The swell is glossy and smooth as an ice cube. Walk past Pier 23 and stop in The Galley for a cup of coffee before going on. The waitress is faded and old and she likes to talk about Jimmy Hoffa, whom she hates. Her calves are lumpy with varicose veins.

"Still working?" Her greeting is always the same.

"Enough to drink coffee. Let me have a couple doughnuts."

"If the frigging Teamsters strike you'll be eating the holes."

"They won't strike."

"The hell you say. Kennedy keeps after that bastard Hoffa, he's going to try and stop the world. . . . I wish they'd put him away for a hundred and fifty years. . . . One of his strikes killed my old man. . . . Dock workers just sat around on their hands for weeks and couldn't get no action and when Charlie took sick we didn't have no wherewithall to do nothing about it. Man like Charlie wouldn't go to no free clinic . . . had his pride, you know . . . said he'd rather croak than take charity." Same harangue every day. She never alters a line. When she bends over, her bloomers show through the white nylon of her uniform.

Take my sandwich down to Fisherman's Wharf during the lunch break and wander along the covered sidewalks past the souvenir shops with their baroque jumble of plaster and glass junk—everything from Saint Christopher to phallic effigies of Coit Tower. Coitus tower. The fancy model opens at the base so you can see a replica of the WPA murals on the wall. *We Paint Awful.* Past the racks of "scenic" postcards, a merry-go-round of sunsets behind the Golden Gate, cable cars creating a hill, crab boats returning with a catch. Alcatraz has a tricky blown-up circle showing a civil servant sitting in his machine gun tower. And there are restaurant cards showing mom and pop and the kids from Columbus, Ohio, eating chioppino in the blue-grotto atmosphere of Alioto's, all staining their napkins with juice and grinning like morons. Past the sidewalk crab merchants with their steaming cauldrons of boiling water and their long tiled sinks with the crabs stacked according to size. Twice a week I spend a buck for a small one and while the man cracks it with his wooden mallet I con half a lemon from the brine shrimp vendor down the way and then go out and sit on the end of a pier and read the *Chronicle* while I eat. Good news on every page.

PATHOLOGICAL KILLER STALKS
NIMITZ FREEWAY

BOMB BLAST ROCKS FELT PLANT:
KILLS SIX

Strange looking through an old newspaper. You wonder if anyone remembers last year's catastrophes or if anyone ever cared. The dead don't care. Why should the living?

EAST SIDE MAN QUIZZED IN
RAPE SLAYING

HOTEL FIRE BURNS FOUR

The President is calling for peace in the Near East and

the gulls pick the broken crab shell out of the water. But nothing, nothing, can spoil my day. The world is a junk-yard overrun by cretins and I don't mind in the least. I am free of them all. The boards on which I sit are warmed by the sun, and across the bay the Marin hills are soft green like old velvet on a sofa cushion.

V

π While I am digging through my box let me dredge up a portrait of Dasha. Never was there such a vacuous creature as my barmaid from Big Sur (currently of Big Sur; recently from four hundred and eleven different places across the map of America). She was a puppet come to life; a rag doll magically transformed. Within her slender body there was only energized sawdust, a dim mind groping for freedom, the transplanted soul of a burlesque queen. "Her life is an illusion," Michael used to say. "She is without mind, modesty, morals, and money. She is a nullity, a cipher, a zero, a blank. She is the great destroyer. A mutation, a cankerworm . . ." Michael overdid it. No doubt he wanted to lay hands on her and was afraid if she kept after him he would. He was a very straight man in many ways.

For a time Dasha worked at the old hotel on Tomales Bay, and I met her there one weekend when I drove north along the coast to see Michael and Rosa and tell them of the wonders of a San Francisco interlude.

Michael was not amused. Rosa told me that a collection of Portrero Hill freaks called the Nicotinic Acids had motored up from San Francisco in a broken-down truck bearing a large, painted sign that read *ne plus ultra,* and they had spent four days tearing the place apart, squirting each other with water pistols, and making obscene gestures to the passing Marin County natives. Michael was, as Rosa said, "tear-assed."

I found him in the barn next to the hotel, nailing up panels of plasterboard on the bare studs of what had once been a boatbuilder's loft. "We're building a gallery," he said. "Having our first show next week. How's school?"

"I quit."

"What do you mean quit?" He put his hammer down on a sawhorse.

"Just what I said, I chucked it."

Michael took a handful of nails out of a keg and poured them into his carpenter's apron. He walked up and down, looking at his half-finished paneling. "How's Ellen and the bambino?" he finally asked.

"I quit that too."

Two helpers came in lugging more plasterboard and Michael had them lean the panels in place along the wall. He showed them a pile of junk in an adjoining room that he wanted taken out to the truck and hauled to the dump. Then he came over and sat on the sawhorse. "You left Ellen and the kid and you quit school." It wasn't a question and didn't require an answer. "So? What am I supposed to tell you? That you did good? Smart move, Ryan?"

"I didn't come for counseling."

"What did you come for?"

"Christ, you're sure in a sour mood. You sound like my father or something."

"I wouldn't be your father on a bet." He sat with his hands on his knees and looked vacantly across the loft. Swallows flitted around in the eaves. The wind banged a door somewhere in another part of the barn. "Man, what's with you anyway?" he finally said. "I used to think that under your nihilistic façade I could see a soul coming, but I'm beginning to doubt. You've been so long committed to noncommitment that I don't think you can tell the difference anymore between your ass and a teacup. What the hell do you think this world is anyway? A Hollywood pipe dream that you can walk in and out of any time an impulse strikes you? A Quaker meeting where you can stand up and shout every time some gas pain moves you?"

"Don't get your dander up, dad. You're going off half-cocked. You don't even know why I left."

"I don't need to. You probably read about it in some Kerouac novel. That's the bit, isn't it? When things get up tight, cut out. When the shoe pinches . . ."

A girl appeared in the doorway of the barn, then came wandering in, posters and a paintbrush in her hand. She had black hair that hung straight down her back to her waist, and she was wearing an old pair of cords and a sweat shirt covered with paint. Her feet were bare. The light from the loft window caught in the gold hoops that hung in her ears. "What do you want me to do with these signs?" she asked Michael. He looked at her for a while, as if he couldn't remember where he had met her before, then said, "Get some stakes or something and nail them on. Drive them into the roadside down a ways from the hotel."

"Which end of the hotel?" she said.

"Both ends. Both ends. You got two signs, don't you? Here. Take this stupid bastard with you and together maybe you can figure it out." He went back to nailing up his panels, and I welcomed the opportunity to get away.

Dasha told me she was from New York. "Rye, New York. That's the place where they forgot to put the *y* on *grove*," she said with a clever smirk. "My daddy is the biggest gut and the smallest mind to ever ride the New Haven Railroad. And he has ridden it every day of his silly life for the past twenty-five years." Not Dasha. No eastern prep life for her. No job with a New York cosmetics firm after graduation. When she finished high school she came west "on account of all them oranges and sunshine and beautiful people. I had to split, you know. New York's a bad trip. Everybody's dumpy in New York. After winter they all look like biscuits with the clap."

Dasha worked at a resort near Lake Tahoe ("up in the groovy mountains"), met some guy who took her to Mendicino ("he had a thing for my body . . . he wanted to paint it all the time"), grew tired of the endless fog and hitchhiked south along the coast to Tomales Bay where Mike hired her to help around the hotel. "It's kind of a drag around here, though," she said. "Hardly any people ever. I'm thinking of moving to Frisco, or maybe Big Sur. I hear it's a scene down there. The thing is, if you don't keep moving you're dead."

She kept moving all right . . . down the road in front of me as she talked . . . like a metronome. Her pants were too tight and her sweat shirt too loose. Keeping my eye on her rear end was like watching a Ping-Pong match.

We found stakes, nailed to the signs to them, and took

the first one down past the hotel and pounded it into the shoulder of the road. Dasha looked sweet and childlike as she held the two-by-four that I was pounding with a rock. The sun was on her face, playing in the golden hoops that dangled against her cheeks. She bit her upper lip between her teeth and closed her eyes against the glare. A portrait of innocence. I wondered if her parents knew where she was.

On the way back she stopped short of the hotel and said, "Let's go check my fish trap. I put it out every morning and sometimes I get a crab." I followed her out toward Michael's skiff and for some reason said, "Your pants are too tight and your shirt too loose."

"Depends if you're an ass man or a tit man."

I nearly fell off the pier. "What kind of answer is that?"

"Sure," she said. "Why not?"

"No. I asked you 'What kind of answer is that?' "

"Take your choice," she said.

Communication with Dasha was never very lucid, but she didn't need words to convey the only thing that was in her mind—when there *was* anything in her mind. I discovered who was the crab in the fish trap when we got out to the shack on the end of the pier, and if she hadn't been so brazen about it, I might have swallowed the bait. As it was, Dasha reminded me very much of a little girl I once knew who used to take her pants down behind a tree and let everybody look. There was something horribly simpleminded about it; an idiotic lust that wasn't even aware that there are rituals for seduction. She wasn't rejecting any code. She simply didn't have one.

Michael, in his newly acquired conservatism, tried belatedly to warn me to stay away from her. "She's bad news," he said. "She's a man-hater. She wants your balls for her trophy case, and don't flatter yourself about her discriminating taste. She'd take on an elephant if she thought it would serve her purpose. Besides, she is very stupid. So are you, by the way. The more I think about you the madder I get."

"We back to that?"

"I assume you came up here to confess, since I've never known you to drop around for old times' sake. You want to tell me why you dumped your wife and child and career? Or did you decide that isn't any of my business?"

"You still sound like my old man."

"I told you, you couldn't give me that role on a platter. It might come as a surprise to you, but it isn't necessary to want something from someone in order to be concerned with their fate. I'm interested in yours. I'm interested in all kinds of aberration."

So I told him, and the more I told him the madder he got. I said, "I dumped it because it was constipating, because it was tying me up in little knots, because I began thinking double, seeing double, talking double, because every time you have dealings with people you become responsible for them, you begin to owe them something, you can't act anymore, you're not free—"

"Okay, okay, forget I asked," Michael cut in. "I heard it all before. I retract my warning about Dasha. Go to her, my boy. You two are a perfect match. You know why she came to California? Freedom. 'Oranges, sunshine and beautiful people,' she says. In her simple, twisted, little mind she was seduced by a dream, by a random spirit that she thinks floats around over here between the mountains and the sea. She thinks that in California people don't have to behave; that there are no responsibilities here; that people just emote and express the freedom of their souls in any freaking way they choose. And you know what happens to people like Dasha, Ryan? She destroys a few souls, seduces a few ninnies with the same fantasies that have seduced her, and then *she* is destroyed. By time. Because someday you have to wake up, man, and look around at reality, and you discover that you aren't a kid anymore, playing marbles in the back lot. One day you wake up and find that you're an old bum with no place to go, and no strength to get there. Old bums are sad, Ryan. Ex-beatniks are just one rung down on the ladder of pathos from aging fairies. So you just keep babbling about spiritual freedom and you keep on scratching where you itch, and one of these days you'll find yourself sucking the dry hind tit of a dead dog, and all you'll have for company is Dasha and her sisters."

"Well, you are probably right about Dasha," I said. "I wouldn't know. But I'm not scratching spiritual itches. I just don't see the point in following a dead-end street simply to get to the end. Particularly when it says 'One Way,' and I'm going the wrong direction."

Michael's sermons gave me the phantods. He was on such a moralistic kick that by Saturday afternoon I had had enough and I drove back to San Francisco without staying the night. The sun was low on the crest of the hills as I wound along the back roads toward Novato and the Redwood Highway. The dairy herds were coming in for evening milking, plodding slowly along the paths they have been wearing into the hillsides for a hundred years. I remember them. I can see them as they move in single file across the terraces of time, their shadows stretching farther and farther away behind them, until they are left to wander the last half mile alone.

VI

π The last to be hired is the first to be fired. I was. I am.
On my birthday I was laid off and it was the only present
I got. I spent the days wandering around the city, doing
nothing, thinking nothing. There was a week of afternoons
in the park, lying on a sunny strip of grass by a bouquet of
rhododendrons or wandering around the zoo. Life is never
in front but just off to the side. I need not look at it or
care about it. When I get bored I go out in the lobby and
buy some popcorn.

At the zoo there is a miniature train that the children
ride: quarter mile of track and it goes around twice for a
dime. On warm Saturday afternoons in March I went
there and rode it for two or three hours. Round and round,
through the tunnel where the kids all holler, listen to the
echoes of other times and places. Sit out on the platform
of the tiny station and eat an Eskimo Pie. Ride around and
around again and again, smiling like an idiot over the

heads of five- and six-year-old children whose mothers look at me strangely. Once in a while Mom gets on with a kid too small to go alone and I feel more at home, and once, when I was eating my third Eskimo Pie, a small boy sat down next to me on the bench and we watched the train disappear behind a man-made sand dune. His hair was blond and he looked very serious and after a while I asked him if he liked riding the train.

"Never been on it," he said.

"Want to go? I have a bunch of tickets."

He looked off toward the merry-go-round where his mother was ministering to his brothers or sisters and then he said "Sure" and we went. The train stopped and a goon in a duck-billed railroad cap took our tickets and said, "Your boy?" and I said "No" and around we went. Once, twice, three times, hollering in the tunnel which tickled the boy so that he could hardly stand it, and when the train finally stopped a fuzzy-looking policeman escorted me out of the park and drove me to the local precinct station. When they asked me questions I went to sleep and dreamed of black swans floating in an artificial lake and in my dream I lay down under a willow tree on the bank and went to sleep and dreamed that an army of women carrying placards came and dumped violet-colored poison into the water and the swans slowly turned white and died. The lilies and shrubs around the shore withered and everything was blasted and dead. The carcasses of the swans rotted in the mud where the lake had dried up.

Did I really dream that? Or did I see it in a movie? Both, maybe. Sometimes I discover that things that have happened to me happened in a theater. After the week at the zoo I used to drive out to Fort Point and watch the colored kids fishing under the mauve shadow of the

Golden Gate. Once when nobody was there Kim Novak came and stood in the breakwater for a minute and then jumped into the bay. Before I could move Jimmy Stewart appeared, throwing off his coat, and dove in after her, and when I went and shouted at him to see if he needed help, two fruits in yellow pajamas with bellboy caps on their heads came out of nowhere and hustled me into my car. I found their flashlights on the front seat when I got back to the produce district.

What I want to say is that in order to disbelieve in time one has to be very conscious of it. I am not conscious of it. I don't care about it. One moment is like the next or the last to me. The tree that the men are sawing up out on the lawn fell yesterday. The tree that the men will saw up on the lawn tomorrow is falling now. The tree that the men sawed up on the lawn yesterday will fall tomorrow. The tree never fell at all. I made it up, and the men too. And myself. That's not cleverness, that's indifference. I am Alpha and Omega, I tell you, and I do as I please with my world. There is no park outside my window. No pine forest with looming dark trees that groan under the lash of a summer storm. The hill falls away for a mile and drops into a Vermont lake. There are maples below, turning orange and red and yellow in the cold October weather. Across the lake a late summer camper is burning trash and the blue smoke of his fire drifts up and vanishes into the blue of the mountain range behind. The mountains blend into the sky with only a faint line to mark their ridges. There are goldenrod and a few white pine with long needles like a shaving brush, and off to the left a white farmhouse and weathered barn.

I spent a hundred mornings, afternoons, evenings sitting

in the basement of the City Lights Bookshop reading
whatever was on the shelf nearest my hand. A paperback
is an unlovely thing. No feel or shape to it worth having.
I'd go to the used bookstores near Jackson Square, wandering, browsing, feeling the old leather and filling my
nose with the must of mildewed covers and old paper.
Once I had a fistfight with an ex-sailor who ran a hole-in-
the-wall shop and accused me of concealing a book under
my duffle coat. He was a tough little Russian Jew who
wound up in the book business because he had spent so
many days and nights in warm libraries during the thirties
that he had come to know what was in them and he told
me all about his life over a cup of strong black tea that he
brewed in the back of his shop after he had called me a
son-of-a-bitch and slammed me up against his shelves. I
hit him with a dictionary and then he apologized, saying
I wouldn't be so angry if he weren't in the wrong.

"Miserable *pishers*," he said. "Beatnik *dreck*. They rob
me blind. Come in and ask for a book and when I turn
around they steal. Last week, yeah, a guy comes in and
I am talking to him and he seems like a nice fella and I ask
him does he want some tea and he says yeah and I go
back to put on the pot and next thing I know he's gone
and my cash drawer with him. Fuckin' beatniks! You ever
read any Jack London?"

I helped him close the shop at five and bought on credit
an ancient but complete set of Mark Twain.

"I give it to you on credit," he says, "'cause I wrong
you."

Close up the night at Vesuvio's drinking beer and talk
ing with an old Filipino painter named Vincent. Inscru-
table as a prune and of a similar color and texture. Vincent
sits in a hooded cane chair (his private box seat); wizened

icon with a pearl-gray fedora on his head. The gloom of the bar and the brim of his hat obscure his eyes and he seldom talks. Ancient, deflated Buddha. When he does speak he rattles like death and I half expect to see his shrouded chair burst into flames. What he says never makes any sense.

"How old are you?" he asks.

"Twenty-eight."

"The river never runs backwards."

"You mean upstream?"

"So you run upstream?"

"I run downstream, but things that float in the water keep overtaking me."

"When the river comes to a cliff you will fall over. Better to run upstream."

"Upstream is where I've been."

"Upstream is knowledge." And he sinks back into his coffin chair and we sit for over an hour without speaking. Near closing time he emerges, takes a cigarette from my pack on the table, and lights it with a shaky hand. "Man lives less than a hundred year. Why do you fret a thousand?"

"I don't understand you."

"Far past and distant future are the same," he says. "Run away from one, run into the other." Vincent puffs on the cigarette and when he exhales he does it so slowly that the smoke steams up around the brim of his fedora and hangs in yellow layers around the crown. "We have a proverb," he says, as I get up to leave. " 'Life is a dream walking. Death is a going home.' " Vincent makes my skin crawl.

I go down to Pacific Avenue and trudge back to the water-front listening to my echo is the deserted streets.

VII

π I do as I please with my world. There is no lake down below or maples turning in the fall. There is only the ocean and a field covered with orange and red and yellow poppies. The blue mountains in the distance are nothing but fog rolling in toward the coast and the camper's smoke is a gray whale-spout as a herd moves south toward warmer waters and the breeding grounds. I can change my scene quick as a slide projector.

On Saturday night Vesuvio's is very crowded—mostly regulars since there is no tit show and no jazz band to draw in the tourists, and the waitress has all her clothes on. A couple come in, hesitate by the door—brief debate—work their way through the crowd milling around the bar, ask if they can share my table. The woman is dark-skinned and long-nosed: raven black hair cut short, almost like a man's. Where have I seen her before? In a dream? A movie? "We live in Palo Alto," she says. No help. Where was it? At Stanford? Santa Cruz? Her appearance, even though hawkish and masculine, is too striking to forget. "I teach painting classes," she says. "Just started a gallery in an old barn in Woodside."

It must have been sometime, somewhere, with Ellen. Ellen with her tubes of paint and dirty brushes and smocks and artsy-craftsy friends. Was she ever at our house? Hard to say; I was home so little. "Do you by any chance know an old painter who's supposed to come in here a lot—Vincent Rizal?"

"Sure."

"My partner and I are very anxious to try and get him to hang some paintings in our gallery. Ellen—that's my partner—thinks his stuff is tremendous and the people around Woodside would pick up on it right away."

Yes, Ed. Truth *is* stranger than fiction. Your old Aunt Effie did run off with JoJo the dog-faced boy from the circus only to be raped in 1947 by King Kong in the back seat of a Willys Jeep. And I did run into my estranged wife's painting partner in Vesuvio's bar on Saturday night, March 28, at precisely 10:47 P.M., and she did ask me to a party in Mill Valley that I eventually decided to attend and there I met . . . Aunt Effie and JoJo. If you believe it don't tell me. But where would we be if it weren't true?

Ellen is dabbling with paints and pots. Playing artist. Building worlds. Starting galleries. Poking around in beat bars looking for kook art that will sell to the old rich and the *nouveau riche* in Woodside's glens and glades. Sell them a pill, Ellen. Sell them a trip into the gallery of their minds. Sell them a strobe light and an enema bag and waft them off to heaven or hell. Some of us need pills and powders. Some don't. Surely they will like Vincent's work, Ellen. *You* do. Swirls of phosphorescent colors, patterned skies, prismatic fireballs, splotches and splashes. Let us feed the constipated imagination, expand the unconscious. Personally, I dig Norman Rockwell.

"Vincent will be along. Sometimes he comes late."

The woman's husband, very conspicuous in a coat and tie, looks around the room as if he thought he might know somebody; spies two lesbians conversing intimately at a dark corner table; excuses himself and goes over to them. He gets a cold eye from the butch but he talks with them a minute and her partner waves him into a seat. His wife says something to me: "There he goes again," or "Here we go again," and then she is telling me about a party they plan to throw in an empty house in the woods behind Mill Valley. It is not clear whether they own the house or simply know that it is vacant. "Paul is going to invite those two dykes, you can bet on it," she says. "That's his notion of a big time. Round up all the queers, male and female, that he knows or can find and throw them all together at a big party. I think he got the idea from Sartre. Would you like to come?"

"No thank you."

"Sometimes it really is quite amusing. And there are always interesting people there—artists, and actors and whatnot."

"I don't happen to be an artist or an actor or a whatnot."

She looks down the ridge of her nose into her glass of wine. "Do you think Vincent Rizal would come?"

"I doubt it very much."

"I know if Ellen could talk to him she'd persuade him to let us hang him in our gallery. His paintings, I mean. Ha ha ha ha."

"I doubt it very much. Tell me about your partner."

She tells me Ellen lives in Woodside and she paints and runs the gallery half-time. She is apparently a lovely girl but she doesn't go out much because she has a little boy about three and a half years old and she still has a husband who is around somewhere but nobody knows exactly where. It's expected that he'll turn up eventually, so Ellen is just waiting. That's her game, all right. Patience, stoic acceptance of fate. Roll your rock, Sisyphus. Smile placidly while the fox eats your liver, little Spartan. Don't try to alter the course of history. Let it run. Wait. "She's bright and pretty and has a terrific figure," says the dark lady. "I don't see why she waits for that bum."

"She say why he disappeared?"

"She doesn't talk about it."

"How is the boy?"

"The boy? Oh . . . well, he's fine. Pretty self-sufficient for his age. Plays around the gallery and you'd never know he's there."

"Isn't he in nursery school, or something? I mean, doesn't he play with anyone else his own age?"

"He pretty much sticks with his mother."

"He ought to have friends his own age. He ought to be in nursery school, for Christ's sake. Start learning how to get along."

She looks at me strangely. A glimmer of recognition? Where have I seen this guy before? "Say, you seem pretty concerned. If you're really interested, why don't you come to the party and meet her? Might do her good to meet a good-looking boy." She gives me a frank stare. "Like I say, she doesn't go out with anybody."

"As I say."

"Huh?"

Paul comes back to the table with Butch and Jane in tow, and we all sit around drinking beer that he pays for and listening to him describe the run-down house he owns near the Muir Woods; a rambling three-story barn with gables and turrets and a captain's walk along the top; buried in an overgrown forest of madrone and oak and redwood. This has got to be a stage prop.

Vincent comes in about midnight and I drag him over to the table and shove a beer under his nose. He sits impassively under the wide brim of his fedora and you can see his eyes only when he tips his head back to drink. Impossible to tell if those bright little slits in his mask actually see anything or if he has tuned himself out and sits placidly in a private, empty barroom. The woman is chattering away at him, praising his art, implying there will be many valuable sales if he will hang his paintings in her gallery. The longer he is silent the more patronizing she becomes; begins to tell him of the art critics she knows. She can get him a big write-up in the Sunday paper. She ups his percentage. She hints at commissioned work. After a while Vincent tilts back his hat and says to her, " 'Butterflies never talk of snow nor worms of heaven,' " and he gets up and goes over to his basket chair and disappears into its hooded darkness.

"Is he crazy?" the woman asks.

"What do you think?"

"What does he want?" she cries.

"Maybe it's what he doesn't want."

"What's that?"

"Maybe he doesn't want to hang his paintings in your gallery."

"Well, it would get him some recognition at least."

"He doesn't care about that. Vincent is a crazy old man. He thinks about death, not about fame and fortune. He once told me it takes forty years to learn to live and forty more to learn to die. You're in on the wrong forty. Galleries and selling paintings and write-ups in the newspapers don't mean a thing to him anymore because Vincent's theory is that we come with nothing and we leave with nothing and last-minute acquisitions are not only senseless but immoral. Leave the trophies to those who can be inspired by them. Besides, he's a lousy painter and he'll give you the creeps."

Paul is describing a party he has given or is about to give and Butch and Jane are exchanging "should we, shouldn't we" glances and suddenly I am very tired of these sightseers from the Peninsula. I get up to leave. Ellen's partner writes down the Mill Valley address and gives it to me with a "hope you'll come" smile and I walk out into the sidewalk press that surges toward Broadway and upper Grant Avenue. Cross at the traffic light and walk in the direction of home. Midnight, and on Broadway people are still stacked up outside the Jazz Workshop waiting to have their skulls rattled by Miles Davis and his group. The strip looks like the main drag of Pamplona when the bulls are running: sailors on leave from their ships, mid-Peninsula businessmen on leave from the wives, college boys all buttoned down and zipped up and swaddled in olive green worsted, looking very dapper with their tight-assed Chi O's and Tri Delts and Kappa Kappa Gambits prancing along on wobbly heels. Outside Dante's the bogus beatniks from San Mateo, Burlingame, Palo Alto are standing around looking cool and dirty in their weekend costumes wondering what bar might let them in without asking their age. A few genuine left-overs from the Portrero Hill exodus are on their way home to expensive pads on the bay side of Telegraph Hill, muttering about the commercial development of the Latin Quarter and recalling the days when Big Daddy Nord ruled the roost in his violet-colored contact lenses and The Place was still the place.

Everybody surges up and down and goes nowhere and does nothing. A school of sardines chased by neon lights; a frantic pen of jackrabbits blinded by the onrushing headlights of party-time Saturday night. Outside the top-less joints the crowds spill out into the street, kids and old men mostly, standing on tiptoe hoping for a peek at a go-go dancer when the doorman opens the door.

Down in the produce district everything is quiet. A squad car cruises by, flashing its spotlight back and forth into the dark doorways, turns the corner and is gone. Two cats are making baby noises at each other in an alley and my footsteps ring off the old warehouse as I pass by. Pause at my door to sniff the dank fog that is creeping up from the waterfront and then inside the warm black building. Flip the switch at the foot of the stairs and walk up in the pale gloom of forty-watt bulbs, up to the third floor and down the hall. Pause again at my door and look back over my shoulder toward the dim landing. In the faded mirror I see a figure standing in the hall, hand on the white porcelain knob of a door that is too dark to be in the picture. Briefly, just before the timer cuts off the weak bulb over the landing, I see the figure become two: twin shapes, one of which begins walking back down the hall toward its creator. The timer clicks and everything is black.

VIII

π I have had great difficulty keeping my mind in focus for any length of time. It wanders. It meets old acquaintances and trots off for a cup of coffee, a glass of beer, a German pretzel, leaving me in the shadows, uncertain of my location, unable to find my way home. On a trip to Tomales Bay I began a portrait of Dasha and ran off without finishing it. There is no finishing a mirage. One can only follow its shimmerings across the desert until darkness swallows its counterfeit shapes. But I will add a daub of color to my spurious waitress.

At La Bodega one night, when I was drinking wine and listening to the impromptu flamenco session at the back table, Dasha came in with some bad news in pea jackets and stocking caps. She had on the same corduroy pants and sweat shirt, but a sarape hid the paint stains and she had sandals on her feet. Her two companions hung their elbows on the bar and watched the guitarists and Dasha caught sight of me and wandered over. "Hey, how are you?" she said, and sat down.

"I'm sneaking by. What's happening?" From the corner of my eye I saw Emanuel, the barman, talking to Flotsam and Jetsam who obviously had no money and were being invited to leave. Dasha was telling me about a job she didn't have and the pad she wasn't staying in, and the Spaniards were whacking through a chorus of "Soleares." "Your buddies are getting eighty-sixed," I said, and she waved at them as they went back out onto the street.

Dasha's interest, it turned out, was not in me but in my living arrangements. She wanted a place to stay while she looked for a job. "When the weather gets good I'm going to Big Sur, but this guy who runs the Coffee Gallery promised me work, so I'm hanging around till summer."

There was a great deal of commotion at the back table as a group of college boys, all wearing regimental ties, brown loafers, white socks, began shouting *olé* and clapping their hands without reference to the *canto hondo* that a Jewish looking gypsy was tickling out of his guitar. A glass of wine spilled. A bottle covered with candle drippings smashed on the floor. Emanuel started over to repress their enthusiasm.

"It would only be a couple days," Dasha said. "I got this girl friend which the guy she's living with is going east, and I can move in there."

"Very small," I muttered. "One room."

A bullfight poster got ripped off the wall and there was loud scraping of chairs as the students tried to make a fast exit. Emanuel nailed them at the door and made them pay for the ruined decor.

"I'll do all the cooking," said intrepid Dasha. "I'm a

groovy cook. I'll even clean the joint up for you. I got all kind of talent. What do you say?"

I didn't say anything. I listened to the flamenco. I drank wine. I reflected on the impossibility of avoiding human beings no matter how hard one tried. I marveled at my capacity for becoming involved in other people's lives without in the least trying. When we left around midnight it was raining.

Dasha might have stayed forever if she had not hospitalized herself two days later. I came back from work early that afternoon. It had continued raining for a day and a half but the sun was finally out and the city smelled good. Fresh coffee and chocolate. Damp wood from the crates on the piers. Every building sparkled and the streets steamed. When I got up to the fourth floor of the old warehouse I found Michael sitting in my room.

"How did you find me?"

"From Dasha."

"Where is she?"

"St. Stephen's Hospital."

"Hospital? How come? What are you doing here?"

"Apparently she couldn't think of anybody else she knew. The cops who found her called me. I came."

"I thought you didn't like her."

"I don't."

Then Michael told me a strange story, pieced out of a police report and a sick girl's testimony.

Dasha had been walking along Green Street on her way to nowhere and she had discovered in the doorway of an apartment building a small cellophane package sealed with Scotch tape. She opened it and found it filled with small white crystals which, in her ignorance, she suspected to be heroin. She resealed the cellophane, put it in her purse, and walked down to the Coffee Gallery on Grant Avenue where she consulted with her friend and prospective employer, "Pearly" Gates. He told her he thought it was methadrine. He was not sure.

Dasha spent the rest of the morning trying to decide whether to eat her find or not. She'd try anything once, but Pearly had disappeared and I was at work and there was nobody to look after her if the crystals turned out to be something poisonous. They smelled suspiciously like Sani-Flush. After several hours of indecision she struck on a clever plan. She bought a package of envelopes, took one, and wrote on the front.

> To the Finder.
> I have eaten half of the contents of this envelope. If you find me unconscious please have these crystals analyzed and administer a proper anecdote. Thank you.

Then she dissolved the remainder in a glass of water and drank her magic potion.

Michael did not say, or did not know, what she had taken, but it was not methadrine. Perhaps it *was* Sani-Flush. A new hot-shot. Two Chinamen on their way back from a lunch break had found her in an alley near Jackson Square, vomiting, nearly dead, and they had called the rescue squad. They took her to the emergency ward at St. Stephen's; St. Stephen's called the cops; the cops called Michael.

"I saw her," he said. "She was still pretty green, but she could talk. She said she was staying with you and I thought you might want to know. Couldn't stay away, could you."

"It wasn't exactly like that," I said.

Michael smiled. "I know. She told me she conned you out of your room. She refers to you, by the way, as 'the nutless wonder.'"

"That wounds my pride," I told him, and we grinned at each other. "What makes you so pleased about it?"

"Maybe there's hope for you yet."

"Why is it," I asked him, "that people are always saying that to me?"

I went to see Dasha once in the charity ward at St. Stephen's. She repeated Michael's story and seemed delighted with herself for having had the courage to bite into the unknown. "Just like Alice in Wonderland," she said. "Only it sure as hell wasn't any wonderland. Man, am I glad I wrote that note. A lotta dummies would of just turned on and cashed in."

Looking at her there in bed, listening to her plans to move to Big Sur ("Come on down. We'll have us a time."), watching her legs move restlessly under the light hospital blanket—it all gave me the cold sweats for some reason. Maybe it was the smell of disinfectant on the ward, or the sight of sick people with bottles hanging over their beds and tubes running under their sheets, or the sounds of misery and pain. Whatever, my head went light and I wasn't sure anything around me was real. I was making it all up again. I looked at Dasha, and it seemed I was sitting at the bedside of a corpse listening to Michael's voice coming out of a long, slowly revolving tunnel . . . *she will destroy . . . and then she will be destroyed . . . by time . . .*

by time . . . by time . . . Getting to my feet was like struggling out from under a waterfall. I was dizzy, nauseated, horribly afraid. If I stayed a moment longer I knew I would never get out, and I stumbled through the corridors, knocking against beds, wheelchairs, patients on crutches, nurses, doctors, all of them turning to stare, to wave their arms, to shout *He is escaping . . . he is escaping . . . stop him . . . stop that man.* Frantically I tore up and down the hideous green halls, leaped down a flight of stairs, more halls, more stairs, things crashing down behind me, the whole hospital toppling in my wake—and then somehow I was out on the street and running full tilt along the sidewalk until St. Stephen's was away behind me and the smell of death was exhausted from my rasping lungs.

IX

π We are going to change the tune here—briefly. A voice from the past: a fiction writer's unfinished attempt to transform fact into fantasy, or fantasy into fact—take your choice. In an old Victorian hotel on Tomales Bay some body sat down on a Sunday morning (was it me?) to write a story about a party in Mill Valley (was it really me?), and I have it—unfinished, yellowing, looking rather dingy and old—in my magic box. (I would prefer more White Horse Scotch.)

I include it only to fill gaps. It is certainly nothing to be proud of, Ryan. Not your best, even if only, effort. I'll do you a favor and retype it, because your spelling stinks.

Melvin Warhole is the maddest man I ever met. Completely out of his mind. His room is directly beneath mine on the second floor of an abandoned warehouse in the produce district; one-time establishment of B. Morelli and Sons, egg wholesalers and distributors who are now either pushing fruits and vegetables in South San Francisco or pushing up weeds in Santa Rosa graveyard. Warhole seldom leaves his room. He exists on nothing, and I assume he sleeps during the day, since he rattles and bangs around all night, talking to himself. The sound of his nocturnal muttering comes up through the floor.

When I first moved in I'd pass him occasionally in the gloom of our ground-floor entrance, but he never spoke then. He seemed to shrink back against the wall, to merge with brick and mortar and a hundred years of grime, as if I were some contagious germ coming to contaminate his pale-frail soul. Until a week ago I had no communication and no very clear view of him at all. He was simply a presence in the building, a dark beard in the murky hallway, a sour smell, a muttering in the dark.

It was a Saturday night, last Saturday in fact, and I spent most of the evening at Vesuvio's drinking beer with a bar-hopping couple from Palo Alto who invited me to a mid-week party in an old house in the Mill Valley woods. I said "No thanks," and took the address just in case, and walked back along Broadway through the milling confusion of a Northbeach Saturday night shuffle to the produce district. It was quiet and deserted near the waterfront and the rock 'n' roll that floated down an easterly breeze from the strip emphasized the hush. A patrol car slowly cruised the street, checking doorways with its spot, and I waited until it had turned the corner before slipping into the old warehouse. Paused on the second floor landing and heard Warhole muttering in his room at the end of the hall: only three words distinguishable, *murderers, abortionists, elimination.* When he heard my steps on the wooden stairs going up to the third floor, he stopped.

It must have been three-thirty or four when Warhole knocked softly on my door and came in. "Hey man," he said, as I jerked on the light and sat up. "I'm in real bad trouble. I got to hide or they going to find me and do me in. I heard 'em in the basement, whispering, plotting. They know my pad, man, and they going to do for me when they catch me. What I want to know, hey, is can I lay in here for the night. I'm bad scared, man. Real bad."

He was. His eyes were wide and wild and he kept grabbing his beard and looking behind him as if he expected the door to burst open and the fiends that were torturing his demented mind to leap in and drag him off to some slow, agonizing death. He stood shivering in a worn out T-shirt, bare footed, his old wool pants hanging off his lean flanks like overalls on a scarecrow. "My name's Warhole," he said. "I'm okay, man, I'm no kook, I'm from Cedar Rapids, Iowa. I just want to pad out in here until they go away."

"Who goes away?"

"The Jewish assassins from B'nai B'rith, man. I'm on their list. I'm marked for killing and I'm dead. They hound me all my life; kept me on the run since childhood; they always just a step behind. Cedar Rapids, Des Moines, Chicago, Denver, Salt Lake, Sacramento, to here and now, man, they hound me, chase me, persecute me." His voice is a hoarse whisper. "The international Jewish conspiracy, man. It starts at birth. They circumcise you. First ounce of their pound of flesh. They going to carve me, man, emasculate me, do me in. Then they . . ." A creak out in the hall and Warhole sinks to the floor, groveling, face in his hands. "You got to hide me," he groans.

What was there to do? He was so crazy that I was afraid if I told him to blow he'd get violent. I could see the morning papers: PARANOID COMMITS HOMICIDE IN SLUM DISTRICT WAREHOUSE. "Okay," I said. "There's a sleeping bag in the closet. Use that and cut out in the morning."

"Thank you, man," he said. "Thank you. You're saving my life, no shit, I mean it."

An hour later I had not gone back to sleep and I knew that I wasn't going to. Warhole lay in the corner so silently that I'd almost forgotten about him until I heard a soft, scraping noise that went on too regularly to be the mice that usually plagued me. He was doing something. Scratching his beard? Brushing his hand lightly over the floor? I lay there wondering and the sound went on—regular, deliberate. Swish . . . swish . . . swish . . . swish. I reached over and jerked the light cord and beheld the Messiah lying naked on his back combing his pubic hairs. He was in a trance. I told him to knock it off; to get the hell out. Nothing reached him. He lay there staring at the ceiling, combing, combing, and finally I turned the light off.

I must have dozed finally because when I sat up again at six he was gone. I didn't see him or hear him again until the middle of the following week.

On Wednesday, while I was at work, I remembered the party in Mill Valley. The whole attraction, as it was presented to me by the couple in Vesuvio's, was the wild collection of weirdos they managed to invite; homosexuals, lesbians, transvestites, a poet's cousin who kept his excrement in mason jars and who would, when moved at a party, perform into his shoes; various artists, photographers, writers, trip-takers from Marin County. It was a real blow-out to watch these people snarl. A zoo party. A nitty-gritty. Not everybody was nuts, a lot of the people there were really quite straight. I had told them I didn't think I'd make it, but by Wednesday I was feeling in the need of something to break the routine, and when I went home after work and ran into Warhole on the landing I thought, "Here is my party gift."

"You want to go to a little bash over in Mill Valley tonight?"

"What kind of bash?" He looked suspicious.

"Just a get-together in an old house over there. A few free drinks and something to eat."

"I'll see," he said, and I told him to meet me out front at seven-thirty if he wanted to go. When I left the building he was waiting.

We drove up Broadway, through the tunnel, turned right on Van Ness down to Lombard, and headed out toward the Golden Gate. "Go through the Marina, man," Warhole said. "I dig the Marina." We crossed the bridge and I followed the directions on the sheet of paper, through Sausalito, left at a shopping center through a viaduct under the freeway and out into the hills to Canyon Road, left again and up through redwoods and oaks and madrones. The dirt road that led up to the house was easy enough to find—there was an oversized mailbox painted red, white, and blue on the Canyon Road— and we turned in and bumped along through the bush until we came on a line of parked cars. "We got to walk," Warhole said.

The house was a hundred yards farther up, and as we approached it I felt like an actor walking on the set of a Class C thriller. Vincent Price on his way to liberate some tasty morsel from the clutches of Count Dracula. The building was under the trees and several of its wings were largely obscured by branches. Candles flickered in the front windows (there being no power) and the large front room where we could see people milling around was aflicker from the fire in the fireplace. Warhole and I went in and I found my lady from Palo Alto.

Why did you stop there, Ryan? The prose isn't much, but you have a character going and a certain amount of interest in his aberrations. Warhole is all right, though a little thinly drawn, a bit two-dimensional as they say in the trade. You could flesh him out; explore his madness. God knows he was mad. Crazier than you or me. Why didn't you finish him off?

"My lady from Palo Alto." Is that significant? Shall I find meaning in the last line before the break? To which lady from Palo Alto do you refer? The one who asked you to the party—Ellen's partner? Or Ellen herself? She was there—in that bughouse, that freak show—looking pretty and wistful, a little tired, a little sad. I need a bag full of expletives and adjectives. None fits precisely. I can't remember anything but shame, guilt, and remorse: the need to say something and nothing to say. I stayed across the room and we were like two strangers, both introverts, both uncomfortable in silence, neither knowing how to begin. In the movies he'd chew his teeth and flex his jaw muscles to indicate great tension and then he'd walk over and say, "I'd like to come home, Ellen." And she would bring her eyes from the floor and look at him softly, glimmer of a tear: "I'd like you to come home, Ryan." But I chewed my teeth and ran off and hid in the bathroom for half an hour composing an explanation, a justification, a vindication and when I came out Warhole was drunk.

He stands on a window bench with the firelight washing his hairy face, his teeth gleaming. He rolls his eyes and shifts his weight constantly from one foot to the other, rocking back and forth before his mesmerized congregation, chanting in a high-pitched voice like a Pentecostal preacher. "I'm here to tell you cats," he shouts, "about the international Jewish conspiracy that operates in this land of America through the agencies of J. Edgar Hoover and James H. Gale of the Fedral Bureau of Investigation—

working hand in glove with the murdering Jewish bombers and terrorists of the organization known as B'nai B'rith."

Ellen is across the room next to the fireplace. In the pale light I cannot see her eyes but I know she is watching me, waiting for me to come to her. Her hair shines in the dusk as if it has some special luminosity of its own. Soft, clean smelling, I used to pull it over my face in the mornings and lie there in bed pretending I was a fish looking up through golden grasses into the sun. Warm there, next to her naked body, skin as soft and pure as her hair. What will I say? What will *she* say? Warhole is between us now. When he is finished, perhaps.

"The murdering Jewish bombers and terrorists of B'nai B'rith are engaged in a national campaign of murder, mayhem, fraud, frame, and poison. They have slaughtered my friends and Hoover his very self has bragged that he will have me killed and my testes displayed in the bullet-proof showcases of the FBI building in Washington, D. C. This same Hoover is an inveterate murderer from the walled asylum of his Jewish headquarters: he gloats at stunting the growth of little boys and girls, and his one obsession in life is to destroy the molecular structure of the brain cells of every Christian man, woman, and child in this continent. His organization is engaged in a national wiring campaign through which they play subliminals that deny us our right to self-determination. They poison the waters of our cities with their chemicals; they pollute the air with their vicious gases; they break down the molecular structure of the brain of every Christian man, woman, and child in this continent. And they incite their black brothers to crime, riot, and chaos."

I cannot go to her until he stops this madness. Or until somebody shuts him up. They are cheering him now. Egging him on. Besides, it is too crowded to reach her. Later we'll go outside and walk. She has moved away from the fireplace, closer to the kitchen door. If she goes out of the room I'll follow and think about what to say later.

"The terrorist bombers have engaged in a brainwashing campaign through the Jewish dictatorship in the mass media, conditioning us to accept their Jewish lies as truth. They circulate the secret lists of B'nai B'rith of the enemies of World Jewry, marked for persecution and elimination, and I'm standing here telling you that I have been on those lists since my childhood. The fiendish J. Edgar Hoover and his FBI henchmen have persecuted me since my very *childhood* and I've suffered beyond *belief* at the hands of an inhuman Jewish conspiracy. The Jews stunted my growth. They infested me with parasites, circumcised me, emasculated me, ran hot pokers into my bowels. They poured acid in my anus and pulled the fingernails from my hands and feet. They lobotomized me thousands of times. They mutilated me, tried to give me brain cancer, hounded me from city to city, state to state, they tried to murder me, destroyed my marriage, injected my mother with syphilis and chancres. THEIR JEWISH INHUMANITY IS A STENCH TO GOD AND JUSTICE AND THE CHRISTIAN RELIGION. They gotta be *stopped*. The Jew Deal begun by Roosevelt and his Jewish police state has gotta be *halted* before the mad dogs strike at every God-fearing, God-loving family in this continent."

Warhole gets no further. He sits down suddenly on the window bench and remains there, rigid, staring, as if

something in his mind has snapped and left him para-
lyzed. There are cries for more, and much cheering from
the crowd, and when I look across the room for Ellen she
is gone. Perhaps it is just as well. What could we have said
to each other if we had had a chance to talk? Warhole's
oration has given me a headache and the wine I have
been drinking tastes sour in my mouth. I move toward the
kitchen thinking, "No more breaks in the routine, man.
It's the routine that keeps me sane. The rise and fall of a
day. Get up, go to work, eat lunch on the pier, come home
at five, go to a movie, go to bed. Don't think. When you
think the fear creeps in. The ground is full of cracks to fall
in and the earth smells of death. Get up, go to work, eat
lunch on the pier . . ."

In a small bedroom off the kitchen Ellen sits in the dark
on a straight-backed chair, her elbows on her knees, her
forehead resting on her hands, her heels hooked in the
bottom rung. Her face is turned away from the door and
her hair still glows with its own internal light. For a moment I watch her as she sits there unmoving, then I slip
out into the cold, California night and run down the drive
like a terrified madman escaping the bombers of B'nai
B'rith.

X

π But I didn't go home. Not to Ellen. Not to the warehouse. I drove into Sausalito, parked at Ondine's, and climbed into the back seat to sleep. When the cops shagged me off at dawn I drove up the Redwood Highway to Novato and cut west through the dairy country toward Tomales Bay. No more Simmons mattress company. I needed a week of peace and quiet at Michael's old hotel to clear my head.

How was it that morning? Exhibit a picture. The inside of my skull is solid green. Fantastic, neon green. My head is a lime. The morning was so sharp and the treeless, rolling foothills so solidly green my eyes ached. I was washed, cleaned out, purified, baptized in the emerald intensity of that morning. The odor of manure when I passed one of the dairy ranches along the road was like frankincense and when I came around a curve and out of a small canyon I fell in love. A cow, brown and white with a soft furry udder, had gotten through the fence and was parked placidly in the middle of the road. I stopped. She stood there, chewing. I shut off the engine. She looked at me with her liquid brown eyes, lowered her head, and mooed loudly. Soft, hairy muzzle under her big wet nose. I wanted to go over and give her a kiss right on her fuzzy chops, but a pickup truck sneaked up behind me and the driver leaned on his horn and scared her into the ditch.

Nearer the sea the hills became flatter and more gradually sloping and the ditches and gullies were filled with laurel, sculptured by the wind. I drove slowly wishing I could drift around forever and never see anyone or any living thing but cows and deer and quail. The road dipped down through a draw filled with overhanging oaks, emerged at the bottom, and joined U.S. 1, running north and south down the coast. Turned left and came immediately into Marshal and Michael's dilapidated old hotel teetering out over the bay on its barnacle-crusted pilings. Home of a hundred good times all past and gone. All-night parties in the abandoned tavern next to the hotel. Midnight excursions across the bay in Michael's boat to swim off the sand beaches on the Point Reyes side. Skinny-dipping off the pier with a hundred different girls and balling in the shack on the end with a hundred more. Lying on the rough boards with a crab float for a pillow blowing a joint. Dark, clean nights with a zillion little glass stars smearing the sky. Water lapping underneath at the rotten old piles. All past. All gone.

And Michael gone too. Gone to a hospital in San Rafael to wait until he died of a cancer that was eating him. His wife, Rosa, very dispassionate, very calm and clinical, told me about it all but I didn't listen. Mortality knocks too close. Death is to be run away from, not faced calmly, stoically. Hide your face, turn away, never look it in the eye. On those dark nights when you lie in bed and feel time creeping slowly on, tick by tick (another night and another and another—how many more?), don't think. Don't think. Turn on the light, read, sing, drink, but avoid thinking. If you can see death coming, you must scream and rant and rave. Struggle. Tear your hair. I could not listen to her going on so quietly.

"Rosa, I want to hole up here for a few days."

"Sure," she said, a little surprised at the sudden change of subject. "All right. Take any room you want. There's no one here but the kids and me."

"I'll pay you for . . ."

"Forget it, Ryan. Just . . . enjoy yourself."

I hurt her. She wanted me to lament for Michael, to hang my head and carry on as she wouldn't do. She wanted me to notice how well she was bearing up and to comment on it, to admire her fortitude, and I cut her short. I should have said, "Who is it here I'm supposed to grieve for? Because the only honest stoicism is indifference and the rest of it's all playacting. You're putting on a façade to make me feel for *you*, not him." But I went up to the farthest room on the corner of the third floor, locked the door, and went to sleep. I dreamed of Heckmann's cabin in Big Sur and woke up bawling like a baby.

I stayed three days on the bay. Rosa fed me and I apologized for my shortness with her when she told me about Michael.

"It's okay," she said. "I guess you thought I was being pretty cold about it."

"I don't know what I thought." I watched her comb her long black hair in front of the hallway mirror. On her way to San Rafael to see Michael.

"It seems I'm kind of a fatalist, Ryan. You know I grew

up in pretty tough surroundings. My folks were pickers and I saw a lot of death and disease and misery in the camps until nothing surprises me anymore. It was so unlikely, my breaking away from a migrant's life, going to school, meeting someone like Mike and having him want me. It's like I knew it couldn't last."

She fixed a large Mexican silver comb in her hair at the back and took her coat off a chair. "Bye-bye, Ryan. I'll tell Mike you're here and . . . can I say you'll come see him?"

"Sure. On my way back to the city."

"Thanks. Be home for dinner."

I heard the car start and then pull off the gravel by the hotel onto the highway. The wall clock ticked in the dim hallway and I was alone with a sad, ancient building.

Help me, magic box. I'm in trouble. Trouble all my life, *and I'm so blue/I just don't know what to do.* . . . No blues today, man, 'cause *the blues ain't nothin' but a good woman on your mind.* . . . AND THERE ARE NO GOOD WOMEN. They are all scum. They are rotten to the core. There is not an ounce of decency in all the women in the world. Donne was right. Turn your back and they're lying on theirs, waving both feet in the air like flags over a stadium. You'll notice that it was Eve not Adam who took the first step. He fell because he was sorry for her, wanted to help out, keep her company. A good Samaritan. A lady invites you to her couch, who is so insulting as to refuse? Who is so graceless, so crass, so heartless to turn down a sufferer crying for help? I am an Adam and I am burning in my private hell for the sins of a companion I never requested. Why did you wait till I slept, sneaky Lord? Had you asked, I might have politely declined and there would have been no Ellen, no Rosa, no

Dasha. And no death. No death. Mole, Michael, the boy. And me. Dead. All dead.

I did not ask her to my room. I said good night after spaghetti and a jug of wine and went up to my tower to read over the story I was trying to write. Closeted myself in the farthest corner of the tired old building full of moans and sighs. Hid away from the knock I knew . . . *I knew* . . . would come at the door. Waiting like a rerun *Macbeth* for a tapping at the gate. Reading paragraphs of one of my stories over and over . . . mind drifting off . . . start again...concentrate..."Melvin Warhole is the maddest man I ever met. Completely out of his mind. His room is directly beneath mine on the second floor. . . ." Her room is directly beneath mine and I hear her moving about, pushing a bureau drawer closed, shoes dropping, a buckle striking a chair leg. "A woman can only live so long without a man," she said at supper. "Especially when she's had one like Mike."

It didn't happen. It *couldn't* happen in a million years. It's not to be believed. Aunt Effie ran off with JoJo and got raped by King Kong. That really happened. But not this. Terry and the pirates gang-banged the Dragon Lady and discovered she was a transvestite. But Rosa didn't knock. Leda and the Swan: Oedipus and his Mom. All true, all true. But not Rosa and her Judas kiss. I made her up and I obliterate her: her cloying perfume, her wriggling tongue and her jouncing buttocks, her sweat turning cold as her tears. I erase her renewed fervor, her sucking, biting mouth, her pants and moans. I efface her. Cut her up like a paper doll—feet, legs, hips, breasts—I notch her ears and slit her nose. She is canceled, deleted, dissolved. She could never, ever, have existed.

No rest. No peace and quiet in the old hotel. I am weak

. . . sick . . . throbbing behind the eyes and so weary I can scarcely drive away. In the marrow of my bones there is an interminable ache and my skin is clammy, chilled. I am hot and cold all at the same time and my voice sounds hollow and comes from a great distance. My body is independent of my mind and I must keep saying, "You are driving a car," in order to feel myself sitting behind the wheel. When I say, "You are driving a car," it seems as if I have not said it, but someone else sitting in my skin. The road I hardly see, nor care to see. The "other one" will keep us on it. He will drive us back through the foothills to the great highway and south through San Rafael, Mill Valley, Sausalito. Across the bridge. Home. Shall I stop and see death lying in a hospital bed in San Rafael? I have promised. He expects me to come: to see him and say goodbye before his pain cuts him off from all other sensations. I have promised. She says he is lonely and exasperated at the time he is taking to die. She got a rise from him when she said I would come. Then he was excited. But what would I say? I detest the smell of hospitals. I get nauseated and faint. I don't know what I would say.

"You are driving a car. Turn off for San Rafael in two miles."

Yes, but what will I do there? Sit by the bed and wring my hands? Ask about the food? Do you need anything? Your wife, by the way, is not exactly in mourning. What do you say to a man with no future? Impossible to talk about the present. For Michael there is no present either. Dead already. His life is a brief dream from which he'll soon wake. I can't go. There is no point.

"You have missed the turn, but it's not too late. Get off at Mill Valley."

It *is* too late, and even if it weren't I couldn't go. I'm weary and sick. My flesh crawls and burns and I am freezing. I need to sleep until my head stops spinning and I can think. I need to get away from people, away from voices; away from questions and answers and dealings. Why must one always have dealings with people? Why do their lives always intrude into mine? I want none of them. They are no concern of mine. I should be like Vincent and sit under a hat in a dark room and look no man in the eye. And no woman, curse their stinking juices.

"Pay the man a quarter. Bridge toll."

"I'm sorry, I don't have a quarter."

"You'll have to fill out this form, sir. Mail it in."

Forms, questionnaires. Name and address. Age and place of birth. Height, weight, color of hair. License number. Marital status. Any children? Not anymore. Not anymore. I had one once, but there was this accident, you see . . . it's a bit difficult to explain because I didn't actually see it happen . . . that's part of the problem. I wasn't there and so I could scarcely be blamed. . . . Hobbies and amusements? No. None.

"Turn here and go up Lombard, and bear in mind that you are driving a car."

Not through the Marina this time? Melvin Warhole digs the Marina. Lying on the long strip of grass in front of the expensive houses whose insides he will never see. Watching gulls circle over the masts of expensive yachts on which he will never sail. Hands off the merchandise, Melvin. Look but don't touch. And if you look too long and too hard the cops will run you in for that too. It's all part of the Jewish conspiracy.

Foggy night in London town. The waterfront seems deserted. Around the streetlights there are jeweled halos and the tires hiss on the damp streets. The windshield is a sequined veil through which I see the orange lights of the Bay Bridge glimmering off in the fog.

Park in the vacant lot at the corner of Front and Embarcadero and walk along the tracks to Drumm. Drumm . . . Drumm. What was that old radio show I used to listen to after my bedtime, with the covers pulled over my head and General Electric's red eye glowing softly against the sheets? Footsteps walking slowly up a deserted street, foghorn in the distance croaking its warning across black waters, steps coming closer, closer, stopping, sound of a match striking. Out of the night walks . . . Bulldog Drummond. Covers yanked off. Smack on the side of the head. Radio removed leaving me in the quiet dark with the eucalyptus trees dripping on the roof.

Footsteps walking slowly up a deserted street. A ship sounds somewhere out near Treasure Island and a cat knocks off a garbage can lid. Steps coming closer, closer, stopping, sound of a match striking. Pause in front of the old warehouse to finish the smoke and then inside the dark warm building. *Déjà vu.* I have been here before. Flip the switch at the foot of the stairs and walk up in the pale gloom of forty-watt bulbs. Pause on the second floor landing. . . . There is something wrong. I am not alone. There is someone waiting in the hallway one flight up. I feel his presence again like a clammy vapor inside my clothes. He has been with me since I left Tomales Bay, riding in the car, watching me from the back seat, running on ahead when I parked. I know it now. He is waiting for me to walk up that last flight of stairs. I am discovered and there is no use running anymore. No use. No escape.

The timer clicks and the hall goes black. I can hear him breathing. Infinite patience. He knows I will come to try

and rid myself again of his fetid presence. Up the stairs
. . . slowly . . . feeling for each one. How many are there?
Twelve? . . . fifteen? No hurry. He will be there. In the
hall? In my room? Standing behind the clothes in the
closet? Or just sitting in my chair waiting for the door to
open and my hand to hit the light switch.

Pause on the third-floor landing and listen to my pulse
beating in my veins. I'm coming. I won't run again. The
hall is empty. . . . I can feel it. He is in my room then. Walk
softly down the worn carpet, feeling along the wall with
my hand until I touch the firebox on the wall. The hinges
grate when I open it and the clamps around the axe have
rusted shut. Tear them away, screws and all from the rotten old wood, and move on down to the end of the hall.
The door is partially open and I can feel the switch with
my hand just inside to the left. Kick the door and flip the
light.

The room is empty, but I feel him again . . . somewhere
. . . close by . . . waiting in a shadow. The light from the
room flows partway down the hall and suddenly I know
that he is back there, behind me; that I passed him somehow on the dark stairs as I crept up toward the room,
and I whirl around, axe in my hand, see him floating over
the landing, teeth white behind the red lips of his mani-
acal grin. With a howl I rush back at him, axe raised. He
comes to meet me and just before we collide I plant the
blade with all my force through the top of his skull. There
is a splintering explosion as he disintegrates into a thousand pieces of shattered glass and I leap down the pitch-
black stairs, out of the building, and into the damp fog
that rolls through the deserted streets around the waterfront.

PART FIVE

I

π I thought for sure I was free. The sign proclaimed it—
BAYSHORE FREEWAY—so I hummed a tune as I barreled
down its inside lane. Going home, with glass in my pants
cuffs and a song in my heart. Going home on the freeway
to paradise. No one-way road for this boy. There are four
lanes and they all point south, so forget it, Charon, your
bucket's got a hole in it. Shriek and groan, dismal spirits,
wretched castouts. My ticket says round trip. Break into a
little song. La te da. Accompaniment by the California
Highway Patrol.

"Officer Durkee, pal. Lemme see your license."

"Round trip, pop. Good till 1970."

"How you got this heap to do a hundred and five beats
me."

"You're looking at greatness."

"Yeah? Well, you're looking at the law so keep your wise
mouth shut. Blow in this balloon."

"Gee, why didn't you *say* it was your birthday?"

"This is going to cost you about fifty, friend. Keep smiling."

Cut off at Redwood City. Hum a little tune. *I sell the morning paper, sir. My name is Jimmy Brown. And everybody knows that I'm the newsboy of the town.* Accompaniment by the Santa Clara County Sheriff's Department.

"Lemme see your license, lead-foot."

"Sure, chief. Say, you ever hear the one about the little Indian maiden, Falling Rocks?"

"No, I never did. You want to step out of the car, please, and put your hands on the roof."

"This little Indian maiden, Falling Rocks, see, got lost and so the tribe went around all over the country putting up signs saying, 'Watch Out For . . .' " Not listening. Rude bastard.

"Okay, buddy. Take it about half speed from now on."

Never knew a cop with a sense of humor. Where do we go from here? Dum de dum . . . *This train don't carry no gamblers, this train. This train don't carry no gamblers, this train. This train don't carry no gamblers, no hypocrites, no midnight ramblers. This train is BOUND FOR GLORY, this train.* And no self-seekers, soul-searchers, paranoids, John Birchers. This train is rolling up the mountains of home. *Just Ellen and me and baby makes three.* Better wait till tomorrow. Can't bust in in the middle of the night after a year gone. She'll think I'm crazy. And after that party . . . aaaaagh. Tomorrow. Cool and rational. Repentant.

To Gunboat Larson's then. Lay up a day or so. *Little mountain home in the hills faraway.* Must get this insane music out of my head. Oaks in the backyard. Lie out in my blanket. "Clear your head with Cuban Red." Next best thing, Michael says, to pure Hash. Scares the boogie men right out of your mind. Winding road, winding, winding, winding. More kinks than a sick snake. Hum de dum dum. *I smell the toilet paper, sir. My name is Jimmy Brown. And everybody knows that I'm the pervert of the town.*

From an omnisicient point of view it's all very clear, very clear. Ryan's battered car tears along the Skyline Road under a dense blanket of fog, skids around the slippery curves, follows the dash dash dash of a pale white line. Under the lee of a thickly wooded hill there is a clear patch of road and his foot presses the accelerator to the floor. Two hundred yards and then back into the soup. Ease off. Put the left front tire on the dotted mark. Near the Saratoga turnoff he slows to fifteen miles an hour and creeps along watching for the mailbox that is nearly hidden in the weeds, a beer can coated with phosphorescent paint bolted to its top. The tracks that lead down into the woods behind the mailbox are deeply rutted and overgrown. An old logging road with a cabin and a few sprawling sheds at the end and a grassy meadow around the house where the loggers have cleared an area big enough to maneuver their trucks. During the day it is a sunny patch of quiet in the midst of a dank old forest.

The yard in front of the cabin is cluttered with kids' toys; broken wagons, a tricycle with two wheels, rusty swing set with no swings, a pile of pipes for a half-assembled jungle gym that Gunboat and Hermit stole one night from a park in San Jose and never finished putting together, a headless doll sprawling out of a badly bent stroller. Along the side in a chicken-wire enclosure three white rabbits (stolen from the Stanford Research Laboratories) hobnob with a flock of bantam hens (donated by a departed writing student who rented the house while the Larsons were in Mexico). And beside the wire enclosure there is a pile of car hoods and fenders to be cut up and welded into sculpture. Gunboat's latest masterpiece hangs from the oak tree; an old water heater with stovepipe arms and sealed beam eyes, Playtex nipples, two dolls legs hanging underneath. The whole thing sprayed with gold paint.

There is no moon and the house is dark and quiet. No one stirring. Put the omniscient mind to bed in the back seat of the car. Lull it to sleep with the soft croak of the frogs singing in the marshy grass around Gunboat's water tank. And the crickets. Thousands of tiny fiddles in the night. A battle of the bands. I'm back in the hills of home.

In the morning he is awakened by a little dark-haired girl peering at him over the top of the front seat. "I know your name," she says and ducks down—peeks through the split in the cushions.

"Hey, that's great, 'cause I've forgotten. What is it?"

The girl pops up again, looks at him without answering. Jaws chewing. Gum? At this hour? "You always have gum for breakfast?" She ignores the question, slides the pink wad into her cheek with her tongue.

"Ryan. Your name's Ryan."

"Oh!" And sadly, "You sure?"

"Yup."

"That's too bad. I had a dream that it was Palinurus and that I was the pilot of a great ship crossing the ocean in a wild storm."

"How big a ship?"

"Huge."

"Big as my house?"

"Bigger. And the storm was really cracking. Thunder and lightning. Waves a thousand feet high. I'm steering along there through the pitch-black night, seeing those great mountains of water every time the lightning flashes, and I start to get sleepy, you know? And pretty soon I just sort of keel over backward into the water and float down through the dark; minnows nibbling at my toes, everything very calm and warm and soft . . ."

"Then what?"

"Then I woke up . . . and saw a little ghost staring at me."

"I'm not a ghost. I'm Anita . . . stupid."

"Ah, Anita, Anita . . . You're sure it's not Aeneas?"

"Yup. You sure have dumb dreams."

He opens the car door with his foot and stretches his cramped legs, sits up, crawls out into the morning sun feeling rumpled and fuzzy-mouthed. Two cars and a motorcycle are parked by the water tank. "What time is it, anyway?" he asks the girl.

"Lunch time."

He walks across the yard and through the back door without knocking. Larson's wife is changing the baby in a clutter of coffee cups and plates on the Formica kitchen table. She stands him up to pull on his rubber pants, brushes the toast crumbs off his swaddled bottom, greets Ryan without turning around. "Morning, sleepyhead. Coffee's on the stove."

He pours a cup and pulls out a much burned and torn vinyl-covered chair. Sits on it backwards. "Wow. I could have slept forever if Aeneas hadn't been bouncing around in the car."

"We didn't hear you drive up. You must have been late."

She starts to clear the dishes off the table and put them in the sink. The baby is playing with the toaster cord, tugging at it, sucking on the plug. Ryan sips his coffee and watches him pull the toaster to the edge of the Formica, tug harder as its feet catch on the lip, finally jerk it off onto the floor. One of its plastic handles breaks and its stuffing spills over the fake brick linoleum. The baby looks around, discovers himself ignored, begins a halfhearted wail. "It was after midnight. I don't know exactly . . . everything was dark."

She puts the stopper in the sink, turns on the hot water, and pours in detergent. Why is she chattering about the baby? Why doesn't she ask where I've been, what I've been doing, why I'm back? *(Did it ever occur to you she might not know you've been gone or care that you're back? Excuse the intrusion.)* Maybe she doesn't know I've been away for a year. Maybe she's not interested in why I'm back. *(You just want a question you can refuse to answer.)* Beat it, will you? Mind your own business. I'm trying to tell this objectively. *(You're losing your point of view. Altering your tone. There are rules in this business, you know.)*

"Where's Gunboat?" he asks her.

"Out in the studio with Gordon and Hermit, and some other greaser who showed up on the motorcycle. I don't know him. Don't think I want to either. . . ."

"How's he been?"

"Okay. Except for the hemorrhoids. He had an operation a couple weeks ago but he's still pretty sore. Go on out and see him and let me do these dishes."

The hallway leading to the studio is as big a mess as the yard. An obstacle course of toys, books, records, discarded hi-fi equipment, unframed paintings, scrap metal; plaster-cast Negro boy in a beanie, black face, red coat, arm extended, cardboard sign hanging from his clenched fist, BLACK POWER: jagged lightning bolt painted the length of the hallway, yellow on a field of blue, small puff of white at the tip surrounding a black BOOM.

Inside the studio Lennie Niehaus plays "Cooling It" with Jimmy Giuffre and Shelly Manne. Stu Williamson on trumpet. Warm greetings from Larson and Hermit. Gordon bows his head and genuflects. The greaser in the corner is oblivious to everything but his dreams.

"Who's that?"

"Who knows, man," Gunboat says. "He fell in sometime this morning. Heard we were good people so he came to see us. First and last thing he said."

"The man is unsavory," Gordon mutters. "He is also very high on magic powders that decay the mind and morals. Full of shit, as it were. I say we eighty-six him."

"Where's your faith, hope, and charity, man?" Gunboat embraces the air. "The cat has lost his way. The world has flung him from its tit and he suckles a pale horse. He seeks our love and understanding, Gordon, our compassion. Raise not the dirty end of your stick to this poor social cripple. Clasp him to your bosom. Rehabilitate him with your tears."

"Rehabilitate him, my ass. You seen his arms? Looks like he's been shooting with a drill press." Gordon flips the record over and sets the needle down on the last band. "Rick's Tricks."

"I hear you had an operation."

"Certainly. Why not? Cut rates at the university clinic. Spread your cheeks, wink the cosmological eye at a class of lovely coeds, let the surgeon have at you with his little tool. 'Just be a minute now, Mr. Grapestake. Gather around, girls. Before I begin I want you to notice how the walls of the Sphinx are clogged by the sands of the Nile. Nasty inflammation of the posterior orifice there, Mr. Grippum, and if you bite my finger again I'll anoint you with gasket sealer.' Yes, man, medical science has raped my vineyard. Vintage year, too."

Lazy afternoon. Napping in the warm grass under the oak tree in the backyard. Waking at three when the branches throw shade across warm shirt and Levi's and a little breeze begins to ruffle the meadow. Walking down in the canyon where the old spruce trees were too much trouble for the loggers to cut. Then back to the house around six to drink Gunboat's Jim Beam and watch him put together one of his famous meals. Boned lamb stuffed with a mixture of bread crumbs, butter, mushrooms, garlic, parsley, nutmeg, lemon rind, salt and pepper, egg yolk. He browns the meat in hot olive oil, stuffs it with his concoction and sews up the hole, puts the whole business in a casserole, and pops it in the oven.

"Takes three hours, ladies, but it's worth it. There are many ways to do in a lamb, as you are no doubt aware. You can shish it or kebab it; you can curry it, hash it, stew it; fry it, bake it, and barbecue it. You can stuff it with chicken livers, pork livers, okra, turnips, and peanut butter. You can even stuff it with old rags . . . that's called lamb ragout . . . ha ha . . . you take the rag out before serving. But there is NO way as good as my way, so hold your breath, ladies. It's worth it. Pass the Jim Beam."

It is nearly midnight when dinner is over. Larson has built a fire in the fireplace, though the evening is not unusually cool. The greaser sits on a collapsing camel stool, staring into the flames, his food untouched on the plate beside him. Gordon and Hermit and Ryan sprawl in the chairs around the hearth and Gunboat clumps back and forth on the bricks, waving his arms, pontificating, smacking his hands. Endless monologue. Man never stops talking. Wound up tight as a Swiss watch twenty-four hours a day. Never finished anything in his life. All his energy goes into his sermons. No time for work. God knows how he lives, where he gets money for Jim Beam and boned lamb, how he can afford the camp followers who are always free-loading at his board. Like me.

". . . I mean I was watching this venerable art critic on TV the other night," Gunboat is saying, "over at Peter Stone's house, and the cat is really a fool, he's a hatchet man. He's ripping apart all the good old stuff and praising the new like here is the jazz we been waiting for for eight centuries. I mean he's showing off junk like I got hanging out in my tree in the backyard and calling it ART. New forms, new directions in the concept of structure and design. Abstract expressionism is passé. Now we got Pop, Op, Bop and Rebop. Scalpel, please, sponge, clamps. Cut away that talent there. Lop off that technique. No skill wanted. SOUP cans, for Christ's sake, BEER cans with faces. You should go out to the San Mateo dump and dig it, man. It's full of great art. And he's got this plastic box on the show, all shiny with chrome edges and a big hunk of bloody meat in it with surgical tubing or something sticking out and he's coming on about textures and spatial awareness and observer involvement and whatnot. I should of invited him to my hemorrhoid operation. Depleted voids. Invisible circles. He's plugging this crap to demonstrate we live in a world of clichés. I don't need to be *told*, man, that we live in an antiseptic, paper, plastic, tin can universe. I can *see* that, and I want to see something else. Something beautiful . . ."

Sometime in the night Larson gives up and goes to bed. Hermit and the greaser have disappeared. Gordon sleeps on the floor in front of the dying fire and Ryan stirs restlessly on the couch; drifting away from Gunboat's voice into the dark tunnel of a dream.

π There is a man on television who smokes Camels and blows up the world. I've seen him in living color on the rec room set. On the wreck room boob tube. Patients and programs carefully selected to keep technicolor fantasies from conflicting with our own black and white ones. Let's not punctuate the drabness of their dreams. Give them the blandest fare. Educational programs; science in action. Still there is much agitation in the wards after TV night. Restless muttering, arguing, sulking, bed-wetting. Not the engineer man who smokes Camels, I bet. Releases his tensions by destroying the landscape. Works off his aggressions in loud noises. BOOM.

There he stands on the ridge looking across the valley. Cloudless day. The sun beats down on his tin head as he surveys a broad expanse of magnificent wilderness; pine-covered mountain looms in the background. He fingers in his shirt pocket and pulls out a weed, sticks it in the left corner of his smile, raises his thumb. Terrific explosion rends the air and the mountain evaporates. Leveled, flattened, gone. "Nothing stands in his way," says the announcer. Man grinning, wipes a match on the seat of his Can't Bustum's, lights his joint. Carburates his toke. Winks at the camera. Squints. Points his finger toward the audience. "Been blowing up mountains ever since I can remember." Hard to hold your breath and talk. "Hate 'em. Stinkin' little hills a' dirt. Get under your fingernails, soil your clothes. Full of bugs and worms and birds and CRITTERS OF ALL SHAPES AND SIZES. . . ."

Man's losing his cool. Beginning to smoke at the ears.

"I'm here to tell ya we going to LEVEL this country. Flatten it down, roll it, tamp it. POUR CONCRETE ALL OVER IT. We going to have one solid three-million-twenty-two thousand-three hundred-and-eighty-seven-square-mile PARKING LOT." Starts to giggle. Has obviously forgotten where he is. Fiddles with his shirt buttons, still tittering. Cut off by master control. No tea head's going to mess up big brother.

Why do we destroy that which we most need and want?

I played with Gunboat's kids all over the hills the tin man forgot to erase. How long was I there? Three days? Ten? Two weeks? I can scarcely remember the month. September maybe. The kids started back to school so it must have been September. Copy of a letter here that I wrote to Ormulum asking to be readmitted to the graduate program. Lied. Told him I had worked out my problems and was ready to settle down. Maybe I thought it was true. States of mind come and go like seasons of the year. Spring's joy is fall's depression. New leaves turn brown and flutter off to become compost. Where is my new leaf now, I wonder? Where is it rotting?

I gave Larson thirty of my last fifty dollars to pay for my keep. Hoped vaguely for a teaching fellowship to see me through the year. Hoped Ellen would take me back and feed me off her mother's monthly donation—if I ever screwed up the courage to go see her and plead my case. Larson bought a live shoat with what I gave him and invited everybody in northern California to his "first annual luau."

"First week in October. Saturday. That's right. Bring your dog. Full moon at its peak so we want a lot of howling mutts to keep the werewolves at bay. Snarling pack of curs around the perimeter of the fire while we eat greasy pig and throw the bones out into the dark to things that slink in the night. Leave your baby home. Might get dragged across the moors by a slouching beast. Bring a jug of wine."

We used to walk every day to the top of a long ridge about half a mile north of the house and stand there with the wind tearing at our hair looking down across the foothills to the ocean. Anita would gather late-blooming lupine to take back to her mother and her brother would roll in the poison oak, insisting that exposure would maintain his immunity. It didn't. I had to admit I wanted to play with my own kid and wondered if he'd even remember me. Still I put off confronting Ellen. I knew Larson has asked her to his luau and I needed time to prepare my speech. Time to think of something to say to the woman I'd lived with for three and a half years.

Days went by. I lay under the oak tree and read *Bleak House*. I lay on the living room couch and read *Dangling Man*. I lay on the water tank and read *Crazy in Berlin*.

One afternoon Gunboat came down from the mailbox and handed me a letter. The tormenter flicks his lash. It pops out of my magic box.

Dear Ryan,

Hope this reaches you. I'm sending it to you c/o Gunboat because Rosa said you were just sort of drifting around again and had no permanent address that she knew about. Gunboat is always a good bet. Everyone falls in at his place eventually and he has his ear to the ground anyway, so I trust he'll get it in your hands.

Enclosed is the recipe that I promised you over a year ago and never got around to writing down. Pot cookies. It's my legacy to you, old buddy, a small inheritance I admit, but one that is sure to bring beauty and eternal joy. As Rosa must have told you, I'm down and the boss is counting, but until the bell rings I'm tidying up my affairs, passing on wisdom (like how to make pot cookies), doing a little meditation on the main event, trying to keep from blowing my mind. San Rafael is a hell of a place to be down. It's the wrong ball park. What I'd like is to take my cot south and fade into the Big Sur coast watching the ocean slam into the rocks we used to dig below Heckmann's cabin. Instead I sit in this antiseptic fun house with three old farts who are so far gone all they can do is bubble and wheeze, getting my morphine from a nasty bitch nurse with a face like a spud nut and a heart like a thistle. The only thing to be said for it is I'm perpetually turned on (though, as I recall, the effects are far greater when you don't need it). Here is the recipe.

> Sift together: 2 cups flour
> 1 tbsp. ginger
> 2 tbsp. baking soda
> 1 tbsp. cinnamon
> ½ tbsp. salt

Cream: ¾ cup shortening
   1 cup sugar

Beat in: 1 egg
   ¼ cup molasses

Sift the dry ingredients into mixture (including 6 rounded tbsp. of sifted grass). Form balls about one inch in diameter and roll in granulated sugar. Place on ungreased cookie sheets. Bake in 350 oven for 15 minutes. Cool. Very.

Sorry you couldn't stop on your way back from Tomales Bay a week or so ago (I lose track of time), but I think I can understand why you didn't. You never were much for the bread and circus bit and this joint is some spectacle. A real Coney Island fourth of July. Gray ladies selling cotton candy and three for a dime cigars, do it yourself roller coasters, parachute jumps right into the grave. Blue Cross freak show with a spade barker. "Step right up folks and see the giant anaconda from the Amazon—the one you see on the television and on the covers of magazines—the one that swallowed the water buffalo and squeezed the life out of the prophet of the Ganjeez—you've heard about him, you've read about him, and now for one quarter of a dollar you can see him ALIVE and in captivity -the greatest killer snake in the world—and while you're inside, ladies and gents, you can take a look at the pig, born in Braken County, Kentucky, with two heads, five legs, and one eye in the middle of its forehead. . . .

And then we got the Red Cross Knight, Ryan. Pricking on the plain, he is. Got a severe dose of clap from it too.

Anyway, I wish you had stopped by for a salmon barbecue and a little glass o' wine. I could have fixed you up with Spudnut, the morphine dispenser. But it would be a lugubrious sojourn at best, and I think I'd have passed it by my-

self, given the opportunity. There isn't much to say when
you come right down to it.

So that's it from your old guru. Keep your cool and remember the old fight song. *Hare Krishna, Hare Krishna,
Rama, Rama, Rama*—or something like that. See you in
the next cycle.

Mike

There is much sadness in a box of yesterday's Wheaties.
Breakfast of chumps and has-been athletes. Michael must
have fixed himself up with the spudnut because he somehow acquired 1,000 milligrams of Demerol. He destroyed
himself on October 31. Another note sent in care of Gunboat. This from Rosa:

Nov. 3

Dear Ryan,

Mike died yesterday afternoon from an overdose of Demerol. I thought you would like to know.

Rosa

Lord, let me know mine end, and the number of my
days, that I may be certified how long I must endure this
life. Help me to unearth something less somber, something
with eggs and cheese and butter, baked in a hot oven,
light and fluffy to the palate. Something with joy, Paun-
chus Palate. Something less leaden than that last bomb, if
you please.

October 31st. Halloween. On the wings of an opiate he
joined the ghosts and goblins tricking and treating along
the smoky streets of Dis . . . where do I keep getting these
abominable images? Dante in a nut house? Virgilian psy-
chotherapy? Why not? *Mene, Mene, Tekel Upharsin.* It is
written on the shit-house wall.

III

π The face in Gunboat's mirror is my own. Cover it with mentholated foam and shave it. Be careful under the nose and around the lower lip. Tender there. Very tender. Cut lips never heal. Every time you smile I bleed.

Snip those protruding hairs from the nostrils. Aaagh. Use something smaller than pinking shears. Tweezers if there isn't anything else but it's going to hurt. Try not to scream and wake up the baby. Who was it went around notching noses? Injun Joe?

A little goozum for the hair. In the secret compartment behind the mirror we have zinc oxide, Baciguent, paregoric (pause for a little swig), Kaopectate, a labelless topical anesthetic for the temporary relief of minor sunburn, superficial skin lesions, and nonpoisonous insect bites, Kip, Mycostatin, Minton's Iron, Mildew & Ink Remover (um, tastes all right but no cerebral affects), Dippity-do, Noxzema, paracyclohexyloxy benzoate sulfate, Pazo ointment, and K-Y Jelly. Ah ha. Slick grooming. *Harmless to delicate tissues or rubber appliances.* (I should hope.) Just a little dab, now. This ain't greasy kid stuff.

Put on Gunboat's tasteless necktie (my God, it's a bedspread), brush the tooth, rinse with a tad more paregoric, and we're off. *Froggy went a-courting and he did ride, ah-hum, ah-hum.*

Let us take it once again from above: from the delicate tissues of the omnipresent mind; from the hairball oracle groomed with greaseless jelly from Johnson and Johnson.

Late afternoon, nearly dusk, Ryan pulls into the Chevron station at Skylonda, a crossroad intersection at the summit of the mountain. Broken tongues of fog lick through the pines and the asphalt shines wet with the mist. Inside, Jesse Boon, Prop., eases off a camp stool next to his kerosene heater and comes out to work the pump. Fat man. The cat's-eye in his belt buckle looks at his shoes. Cold cigar is sodden and limp. He cranks the meter, removes the gas cap, drops it, bends over to pick it up, drops the nozzle, retrieves both at once, gets tangled in the hose. Too much sweet port, rum-dum. Finally starts the gas flowing and walks around to smear the windshield.

"You know what they call the Italian navy?" he says.

"No. What?"

"Chicken of the sea." Brown-toothed cackle. He pushes the plunger on the Windex bottle and sprays his hand.

Ryan climbs from behind the wheel and walks around the front of his car, stretches, inhales as much of the moist air as he can hold, and lets it out slowly through pursed lips. In a clearing behind the station, backed by a black wall of redwood and pine, there is a collection of wrecked cars towed into Jesse Boon's by the Triple A; twisted heaps of torn metal, and broken glass, collapsed axles, wheels canting in crazy deformity. Scarred monsters that were once the pride and joy of Tom, Dick, and Harry from Palo Alto. Foreigners from the Peninsula who sucked up too many suds in one of the cozy roadhouses along the twisting mountain road. Discovered too late that the tiger was in the wrong tank.

"Be three sixty-five," says Jesse.

"Nice backyard you got," says Ryan, fishing in his wallet.

"Ain't that a doozy?" says Jess.

He coasts down the western side of the mountain, through patches of fog, past the Homer Ranch and the Silver Spur Lodge, through La Honda with its hopeful neon lights and deserted bars, and out through the rolling, treeless pasture land that ends in a fringe of artichoke fields and the sea. The oaks on the hills look like tiny sponges, little clumps of green on endless, barren dunes: branches and trunks indistinguishable in the closing darkness. Once before, years and years before, I came on this road at the same time of evening and saw the trees thrashing in a macabre dance. The first threatening vision of a world behind the world that Tom, Dick, and Harry see. First glimpse into the pattern and structure of voids. Buzzing in my head and a voice suspended outside my body. Actor and audience no longer one but two; two distinct creatures. Violation of unity. Violation of reality. But I have learned since then. Reality has nothing to do with past, present, and future; nothing to do with tasted, touched, seen, and heard. I have learned much. I am unhinged. And Ryan, poor fool, thinks that he can murder a voice, a vision, a reflection; thinks that he can run away and hide in the arms of a deserted wife who is scarcely prepared for the second coming.

He turns left on the coast highway and drives for several miles along the ocean. The moon is rising out of Santa Cruz and the dogs at Larson's luau will have reason to howl. From the top of a hill he can see its reflection off a line of cars parked a sloping half mile beyond. He puts his Ford in neutral, shuts off engine and lights, coasts down through the moon-washed dunes. All quiet but the hum of tires and the surf. Old memories in the air of nights on these beaches with Ellen and Mole and nameless, faceless girls from Stanford. How long since I was an undergraduate and the world seemed assured? Until you're a senior, the next year can always be predicted. Pity we can't stay students forever. Ten miles south the scraps of Mole's dismantled MG still lie at the bottom of a canyon.

Ryan parks behind the cars on a strip of packed sand. A light mist is still falling but he can see the pale line of breakers as they roll in on the beach below. He slides from his seat and walks up toward the bridge where a tide river flows in and out of the sea. Crossing the road, he goes down the bank and follows the stream through the dunes toward a fire that is lighting up the sky two or three hundred yards inland; flounders in the soft sand, slips, curses the darkness in the hollows. The shouts of the fire-builders break through the damp calm and a light steam rises off the water. From the top of the last dune he looks down into an amphitheater shaped like a horseshoe. A driftwood fire blazes in its center, fifteen feet in diameter, twenty feet high. Logs the size of telephone poles, and whooping troops dragging up more all the time. Eight or ten dogs (Gunboat's request) snarl at one another and race around the open end of the bowl, and Larson, without shirt or shoes, lectures to no one in particular from the top of a log.

"You ought to pay more attention to dogs, you people. Watch them closely, observe their habits. They got all kinds of scenes going. Like they got this gland, see, that flavors their urine with a particular smell . . . like fingerprints, no two alike . . . and when you see 'em running around there like Paul Revere, piddling on every Middlesex village and farm, what they're doing is they're staking out their pad. . . . Like the mutt that just pissed on your plate, Gina, is just letting you know from now on it's his." Great guffaw. Falls backward off the log. The girl addressed chucks a rock at a circling hound and throws her plate disgustedly into the fire.

"Funny thing about dog fights." Gunboat back on his pulpit. "I seen lots of men get bit in 'em but I never seen a dog hurt much. . . ."

Ryan slides down into the circle of firelight and Larson breaks off with a yell. "Aaaarrg. It's Ishmael come looking for lost quahogs in the alien corn." Falls off his log again, clutching his naked breast. Around the fire thirty or forty people are milling, eating sandy chicken and drinking wine in paper cups. More chicken in foil wrapping roasts on a bed of coals raked from the flames.

"Just in time to do your stint with Elmer Fudd," Gunboat says, crawling over.

"Who's that?"

"The little piggy that went to market, man. Over there." Points toward the shoat which is spitted over a separate fire nearer the water, eyes open, pike protruding from its neck, tennis ball in its mouth.

"I couldn't find an apple," he explains with a shrug, "so

I ask myself: 'What would Julia Child do?' And from out of the firmament comes a voice clear as crystal, 'USE YOUR IMAGINATION, ASSHOLE. . . .' I raise my arms in supplication and fall upon my knees: 'Julia, baby, there is nothing in the wilderness but sand. Give me a sign. . . .' A loud cracking fart rends the atmosphere, but I don't dig the message, so I rip off my shirt, shave my head, sprinkle dust in my eyes, and go off to expostulateth with my judge and maker. . . ."

"Is Ellen here, Gunboat?"

"Man, I was just getting to the best part. My blasphemies. My repentance. Marvin Bildad shows up with a tennis racket and a can of balls. Renewed confidence . . . especially in Marv. Broke his heart when he found he wasn't at Forest Lawn, but he's happy now making sand pies with the kids. . . . No, she's not here yet. Be patient. She said she's coming. What is it makes you so impatient to get back with her anyway? You don't find freedom so good?"

"Someday you have to wake up and look around at reality. I'm not a kid anymore playing marbles in the backyard. Freedom is a seductive dream. Leaves you sucking hind tit, a random spirit."

"Ah! Yes! Certainly! The very thing that piggly-wiggly said to me just before I slit his throat. Do be a good lad and relieve Gordon with his little nightmare. He's so juiced he's talking to it. Busted down and wept when its eyes popped open. Says it looks like a newborn babe." Gunboat wandering off to attend to the chicken, waving his hand vaguely in the air.

Gordon squats by the suckling pig, prodding the coals with a long stick, beer can hanging from the fingers of his left hand. He has a toy fireman's hat of red plastic on his shaggy head and, like Larson, he is shirtless. Droplets of grease explode in the shallow pit. Sweat runs glistening through the doormat on his chest. Altogether absurd figure. A dancing bear. A fugitive from Ringling Brothers.

"I'll spell you," Ryan says.

Gordon keeps poking with his stick. "It's very sad, man. It's very sad indeed." He turns a doleful eye on Ryan, lower lip hanging. "I feel like a cannibal."

Ryan walks around the shoat. Studies it fore and aft.

"Does look a bit human. Supposed to taste a little like man meat too."

"I could *never* eat it. *Ever.*" Gordon says. Quick slosh of beer to wash away the taste of his thought. "I warn you, man, don't look it in the eye. It's got a soully expression that'll hang you up. Puts you in mind of Amelia Earhart." He stands up stiffly and totters away toward the main fire, hat like a bird nest on his wiry thatch.

The mist rises more thickly off the water and the wash of its tiny waves seems closer. Tide must be coming in, dumping cooler water into the channel. Damp night but warm in the bowl. The fire is a blast furnace. Behind its smoke the moon is orange—like poppies—like an unpurchased beach ball—like the morning sun through a window in the future. In the middle of this volcano sits the poor pig roaster, turning new leaves as fast as his spit, looking back on chaos, looking ahead toward order; deluded, demented, dissembling himself with false hopes and hollow promises. "I will play it straight. I will accept and live up to my responsibilities as husband, father, scholar. I will *be* Tom and Dick and Harry. I will punch my time clock, be faithful to my wife, play baseball with my boy. I will support the PTA and the Little League. It is right that I should do this because social ritual and the laws of the tribe have been arrived at over hundreds of years of trial and error and there is no such thing as absolute freedom. It's Hammurabi's Code, for sure. Step on a toe and get yours stepped on. Make others suffer and you'll suffer yourself. Live by the myths."

Ass. Patterns are not broken so easily. To understand a problem is not to solve it. Look back with a clear eye and you will see your bright future shining before you. Shining off the glassy swells at Point Sur. Glint of sunlight off an orange ball in the kelp. Blood on the rocks where the bluebottle flies are swarming.

IV

π Where the red and white corpuscles are swarming in the overheated pipeline to the brain, jamming the exits, clogging the aisles. Molecular riffraff littering the hall and clapping for the show to start. Pulsing rhythms behind the stage curtain as the bongo drummer exchanges licks with a black ape on the Congo. Perhaps it is the half gallon of wine he drinks in a toast to the hour of reformation. Perhaps the paregoric he drank in salute to his image in Gunboat's bathroom. Perhaps the superiority he feels toward the unhappy-looking graduate student who accompanies Ellen into the circle. Black knit tie, blue blazer, brown loafers that sparkle in the firelight. "Should introduce him to Marvin," he thinks. "Tennis anyone?"

Gunboat is solicitous. Dances around half naked, offering wine, a foil-wrapped potato, a greasy chunk of pork rib. Drags Ryan over and introduces him: "Mr. James O. Brown, Ryan. Assistant prof in the Philosophy department at the university, I believe." The man nods and tries to

smile with potato in his mouth. Not a student then. A
bright young man on his way. No doubt he is wondering
why he didn't take Ellen to the Kabuki play in San Francisco and a late supper at Fleur de Lys, instead of letting
her drag him out into this frantic mob.

"How do you do, James O. Brown," says Ryan. "I hope
you're enjoying my wife."

The man comes undone. His paper plate tilts and pork
fat runs on his gray flannels. Tries to speak, "I didn't
realize . . . that is, I didn't know Ellen was . . ." Too mealy.
Looks at her for help. Who is this madman? Notices the
grease on his pants and begins to rub it frantically with a
napkin. "I see my colleagues need assistance," Ryan says.
"Excuse me, please. I hope you enjoy your potato too."
He joins a howling mob of drunks trying to topple a twen-
ty-foot log into the fire. They get it on end, give it a heave,
and it smashes in the center of the pile. Sparks shower
over the bowl and there is much screaming and cursing.
Gunboat attempts to run up the log in his bare feet, makes
it halfway, leaps out over the flames and onto the sand.
Loud cheering and cries for an encore. Others join in and
it becomes a game—officiated by Gordon in his plastic fireman's hat. From down by the water Marvin spies the fun
and abandons his sand pies—tears up the sand crying
"SEMPER FI, you muthah's, E PUBIS EUNUCHS."
He runs full tilt through the litter of plates, cans, wine
bottles, sprawled onlookers, and straight up onto the log.
"Look, Mom, no hands . . . no hands." He flails toward
the top, teeters, tries to leap but loses his footing and
plummets into the burning fringe. Scrambles out, yelling,
pants smoking in a dozen places, hands and feet seared,
smacks at hot coals caught under his toes. Yowls with pain
and rolls on the ground. Gunboat leaps to his stump, cups

his hands, and shouts into the night, "Will Dr. Killdear please report to the east gate ticket booth. Is there a priest in the crowd? A PRIEST, A PRIEST. LAST RIGHTS, SACRAMENTS." Hermit hoists Marvin pickaback and with Gordon's help carries him off into the dunes toward the cars. The troops sober. Head back to the wine jugs. Ryan turns to look for Ellen, but she and her well-pressed man have disappeared.

He walks away from the fire feeling . . . how was it? . . . blue? Definitely blue, yes, but more blue-green. Blue-green paisley. Dizzy in technicolor. Worse than dizzy. Sick. Full of butterflies and bumblebees. Full of little boys on their way to the dentist. Full of impacted wisdom teeth. The last-chance bungler watching time run out through the broken bottom of an hourglass. It occurs to him with a sudden force that she is seeing other men, and it makes him nervous and impatient. He smacks his brow for lack of a better gesture. "What a fool. What did I think? That she was going to sit around cooling her heels while mine smoked down the highway? Wait around forever on the chance I'd drift back?" He feels frustrated and jealous and helpless, loose in his bowels. For the first time it occurs to him that she might not *care* if he came back. "Who is that philosopher anyway? I wonder if she's sleeping with him?"

He walks along the shore until the path narrows and disappears into the water, then climbs the bank and continues along through low-growing succulent. At a rock outcropping he sits and flips pebbles into the stream and tries in vain to think of some course of action that will exhibit his supreme indifference to Ellen's departure: finally tosses his remaining pebbles at the water in disgust, and starts back. A shore bird flaps off across the channel as he slides down onto the path and the noise of the party drifts up with the sparks from the bonfire behind the hill. The moon has risen higher but the hollows are still black.

The path turns in from the bank and wanders through the dunes and as he rounds a corner he sees her framed on the sky, ghostly, her blond hair absorbing the moonlight and casting off shimmering waves of its own against the darkness. She is seated at the top of the hill and when he reaches her he has to touch her to make sure she is not made of paregoric and wine. "I thought you'd gone back . . . with your boyfriend." Wonders why he added that.

"No." And then, "He felt out of place and I walked him back to his car."

What is that? Confirmation? She doesn't deny that he is her boyfriend. She might at least say, "He's just an acquaintance, just gave me a ride out here." What am I? Insane? This is my wife. I am married to this woman. Or rather she is married to me. Boyfriends are for the unmarried. Maybe I'm the only one who remembers. Maybe we *aren't* married. I could have conjured that notion like a hundred others I've pulled out of my magic box. "What's the matter? He get too much sand in his potatoes? Pig stick in his delicate craw?" Why do I insist on being snotty?

"Please let's not play this game. Let's not quarrel. May I have a cigarette?"

I insist on being snotty because at this moment, above all other moments in eternity, I should not be.

He fishes a broken Pall Mall out of his shirt pocket. "Best I can do. I'll split it with you." That's the boy. Share the wealth. Be generous. Take the small half. Make like the ads on television. Boy and girl enjoying their Winstons down by the greenwood sidie-o while a peppy trio sings an illiterate slogan in the background. "I'm glad you stayed. I wanted to talk to you."

"I gathered you did."

This isn't going quite right. A bit too cool there. "What made you gather that I did?"

"Gunboat made a point of telling me several times."

What the hell? Larson is now John Alden? Maybe he's been sleeping with her too, the insidious bastard. Why doesn't she ask me where I've been, how I am, what I've been doing? Why doesn't anybody ask me? Did I dream up a year in San Francisco too? Simmons mattresses, Warhole, Mill Valley, Rosa, Michael? The whole thing an idle vision wandering through my skull like a half-remembered picture show?

She digs a hole in the sand and drops the butt in it; smoothes it over, pats the top. "What did you want to talk to me about?"

"Now who's playing games?"

"I don't know. You are, I suppose. You have been all your life. I can guess what's on your mind, but I don't really know."

Still being a hard case. Not going to open herself up for anything. Going to play it calm and reserved. Tell the little boy that he hasn't eaten his vegetables so he can't have his dessert. This isn't going quite right. Better to break the solemnity.

He rolls down the hill . . . wheeee . . . throws handfuls of sand in the air . . . scrambles around on all fours. "There are werewolves about, you know. I hope you're armed."

"Quit being a fool."

From his knees down at the bottom: "Hey baby, didja miss me when I's gone?"

A shout goes up from the fire-builders as they heave another log onto the pile and a tower of sparks explodes into the sky. Did she answer then? Did I miss it? Why this long pause? "Well, did you?"

"Yes." She says it slowly. "I missed you."

"A-hah! 'At's my girl. And was ya faithful to your old sugar-snack poppa?"

The wind blows a little powder of sand down from the crest of the dune and it cascades around his knees like a miniature avalanche. This phony joking is worse than being serious. What holds her back now? The dentist unhinges his drill and the butterflies take flight. The boy braces himself in the chair against the first touch of the bit.

"You were gone a long time," she says.

"Does that mean no?"

"I guess it does."

If we concentrate on the intervaled swish of the tide in the channel as it washes across the pebbles below the bank, we will perhaps not feel. If we focus our attention on the texture of sand under our hands and feet, we will perhaps be aware only of the external. If we converge the tactile, auditory, olfactory senses into one intense revel of sensation we will perhaps create an internal vacuity that will save us from pain. The mind will be clear and blank. The queasy thrill will pass away, the heartbeat will return to its normal count. Perhaps not.

Ellen sits on the dune above him, offering nothing more. He wishes vaguely that he had another cigarette. After a bit she says, "Does that surprise you?" And when he fails to answer, fails to trust his voice to pronounce *What you do is your own business*, she answers for him. "I guess that it does. I'm sorry."

He lies back on the sand at the bottom of his private

kiva and looks at the dark spots on the moon. Funny, funny, funny, funny. Only he is not laughing. You think you know what you think you know and then you discover you don't. Theories of freedom are for men only. Surprising that discovery should come so late, it's hardly a new idea. When men are unfaithful, women weep. When women are unfaithful, all Troy burns. Not funny in the least. As Gordon says, it's all very sad, very sad.

And whose turn is it now? I'm stuck in the same old rut with a hundred things to say and no words or ways to say them. No courage to show a weakness. Only the weakness of a façade that I maintain at all costs . . . even a wife and child.

"I'm getting cold," Ellen says. "Do you want to go back by the fire?"

He gets to his feet, climbs the hill again, and follows her along the path. As they near the open end of the bowl she stops and turns to him. Hands in the pockets of an old pea jacket. White turtleneck sweater shows her tan even in the dark. "I'm truly sorry, Ryan. I am." She looks straight into his face and he begins to shuffle. "I tried, I think, before you left. I tried hard to be whatever you wanted me to be, but it was just silly. I know that now. I never was real to you, I never was a real person, and you just blotted everything I did or tried to do for you out of your mind. I think you even married me because you somehow felt guilty about what happened the night Milton was killed, though I didn't see that then. You made it clear enough later. Even when I *did* understand I thought I could make us work, but . . ." Now she kicks at the sand. "Oh, what the hell . . . I didn't come here to say all this. I just came to say no to what I think you want."

"And what is it you think I want?"

"It's funny how I always do the talking, don't you think? . . . You never commit yourself to anything."

"I was going to but I didn't want to bust in on your soliloquy." Poisonous belch. Taste of metal in my mouth.

"Oh Christ," she says, turning, walking away toward the fireside revelers. I am left with heartburn and heartache. I am peering at ridges on the banks of the imitation river while the sand I have been clutching in my hands runs out through my fingers.

V

π At midnight, standing by the burned out pit where the pig has been spitted, he remembers the boy. A new approach. An entree. She must let me see the boy. Perhaps I can take him to the zoo. Ride the train around and around; holler in the tunnel; eat Eskimo Pie and feed peanuts to the elephant. Bring him home with one of those Mickey Mouse balloons or a plaster bird on a stick or a Giants pennant for his room. Help Ellen tuck him in bed and read him a story from Dr. Seuss while she bakes a soufflé and chills a bottle of Souverain's Green Hungarian—the way we used to do a long time ago. Maybe she'll let me take him to Gunboat's for a weekend to play with Anita and Charlie, or down to Big Sur at Thanksgiving, with Larson's latest inspirational group: "The Friends of Michael." First annual pilgrimage to the country he loved so much and will not see again. Maybe she will come herself and we will be reunited walking through the fields of poppy, watching the ocean pound the ancient coast, feeling the spray lick across our faces and dampen our hair. I'll make it up to her. And to him.

He walks over to the log where Ellen is helping Gina pack up the leftover chicken. "You have a ride home?"

"Gina said she'd drop me off."

"I'll take you if you want."

"There's no need. Thanks."

"There is need. I haven't yet said my piece."

"It's only thirty miles over the mountain. You think you'll have time enough?"

"You sure are determined to put me down tonight."

She looks up with a little smile. Encouraging? Hopeful sign? Softening up? "Nobody has ever put you down very successfully." In the firelight her blond hair turns reddish gold. Once I could bury my face in its softness. Smelled like flowers, like clover.

Larson's wife asks Ryan to bring along a knapsack of potatoes, follows Gunboat off along the path. Ryan shoulders the load with one strap and takes Ellen's hand. She doesn't resist and he leads her through the dunes toward the cars. As they climb from beneath the bridge and start across the road she stops him once again. "Please don't ask me about . . . what we talked about before," she says. "If it ever seems important that you know, I'll tell you. But right now it isn't important and I don't want to discuss it. Okay? Please?"

He drives slowly up the coast, watching the reflection of the moon across the water. A broken ribbon of surf shows the end of the beach and the start of the Pacific. Occasionally a wave crests far out beyond the breaker line—a quick flash of white against the dark sea. Inside the car it is warm and the heat feels good after six hours on the dunes. Ellen rests her head on the back of the seat, just as she did nearly ten years before when she came home dizzy and weak with a gash on her foot. Felt dizzy myself then, from a long day in the sun, from the smell of blood and antiseptic in the car, from the musky perfume of her hair. Felt disjointed, half euphoric, half sick. Now it is only a prickly fear and a weakness in the stomach—a sense of strangeness about Ellen that can't quite be explained or defined: a new composure. Something in her relaxed posture in the warm quiet car, in the way her hands lie motionless in her lap, in the way her hair falls across her cheek as her head rocks slightly on the back of the seat. She is enjoying the moonstruck night, the motion of the car, the hot air from the heater blowing on her feet. She is at rest. There is no tension in her. The turmoil that churns in other guts is as foreign to her as hatred to a newborn baby. She seems simply unmoved anymore by the chaos that has always surrounded her life, as if none of its pains and sufferings, not even its joys, can penetrate her consciousness strongly enough to make her feel. She has a new façade. She is placid. She is an accepter of whatever comes along. She blows with any breeze, never questioning its direction or mood. My God, where did she learn such a part? Who taught her this role? I know the lines very well. They are easy to learn. Very little to memorize and no interpretation needed. Simply ask moral judgment to step out in the wings, ignore commitment when he prances around the stage, smile blandly when spiritual freedom rapes you in the orchestra pit. Ellen has learned well. I know why she has never asked how or why or when or where. Not because she is a stoic but because she is depleted of curiosity. She simply doesn't care anymore what happens beyond the range of her sight and hearing.

The unknown doesn't interest her. But it's a dangerous role, Ellen. It's the first and the last you'll ever play, because once learned it can never be forgotten. The spirit gum solidifies and the mask sticks forever. Oh, it's appealing, very appealing. It makes you mysterious, intriguing, superhuman. It will make you seem like some mystical creature partaking of the timeless, spaceless order of the universe rolling around in its eternal cycle of birth and rebirth. Why should you care about anything? Your life is forever and you will see it all again and again. A million years of evolution have conditioned you for indifference. You are the collective soul of all who have gone before and will come again. I know the part well. I wrote the script.

They drive to the summit without speaking. Ryan turns left and heads north along the Skyline. At Brock's Inn he stops for a pack of cigarettes. "You want a beer or anything?" She shakes her head. Smiles dreamily in the green glow of the instrument panel.

From Brock's he turns onto Kings Mountain Road and winds down through the redwoods toward Woodside. The lights from the Peninsula flicker through the trees until they get close to the bottom. Then the foothills blot out everything but horizon glow. Pine and redwood become eucalyptus and acacia. The pungent compost smell of the mountain turns to tar weed and oat grass. Time is running out.

"You'll have to tell me where to go. I've never been to your house, you know."

"Turn left at the Country Store. It's up in the woods behind the Peanut Farm. Sounds funny, doesn't it. You've never been to my house."

"That's one of the things I want to talk about. I'd like to."

"I told you it would take thirty miles."

"It hasn't. Quite. How about it? I'd like to see the boy. He is my son after all."

"You used to tell me he wasn't. . . . Turn here."

He jerks the car around onto a side road and steps irritably on the gas. The road dips and veers to the left, starts up a long hill. "The house is at the top," she says. "Where the light is." He pulls into the drive and shuts off the engine. Desperation. Time *has* run out and he is still floundering. Can't believe she is so calm. Might as well be poppa bringing her home after the junior prom. "I love this old car," she says. "A lot of things began here. Wonder it still runs." She opens the door and slides out and they walk up to the porch together. Inside, the baby sitter hears their steps and begins to gather her things—waves at them through the window.

"Ellen, wait a minute." His turn to stop her. Has to hurry but he can still get it said. She interrupts.

"If you really want to see him, Ryan, okay. But he needs a father, not an occasional bum who drops around to make believe every few months—every time he can't think of anything better to do. If you want to work out seeing him on some regular basis it's all right with me, but if you let him down, like you've done to everybody and everything else in your life, I *swear*, I'll see you fry in hell for it." She looks into his face again, searches it. So there is something stirring in there. Maybe it's not too late.

"I won't let him down," he says.

The yard is full of leaves. He scuffs his feet through them as he walks back to the car. A great weariness seems to surge up through the marrow of his bones, but his head is still light. There is hope for me yet, he thinks. All's for the best in this best of all worlds.

Woodside is dark as he guns the old Ford along toward the La Honda road. The moon scuds behind the tinsel leaves of the eucalyptus that border the black unlined strip of asphalt. A coon, crouching in the shallow ditch along the shoulder, debates a moment when he sees the onrushing headlight, decides to try his luck, changes his mind in midstream, and gets smashed for his timidity.

Back at Gunboat's a fire is crackling in the fireplace. Gordon and Gina are piling records on the changer and Bob Dylan is singing. Larson, full of wine and pig and roasted potatoes, is just beginning to tune up. " 'Times they are a-changin'.' Marvelous profundity. Where did he get such insight? Three hundred million years ago one of my ancestors crawled out of the reeking ooze of a swamp and Bobby Dylan has just discovered the principle of mutability. What an acute apprehension of the scene."

"Yeah, fan*tas*tic," says Gina, nodding, eyes closed.

"Hair like a clump of pampas grass, walking around putting down squares and they lapping it up like dogs after pig grease and howling for more. Rummy kid was still messing his diapers when I bought me my first pair of sandals and a hock-shop guitar, and now he comes on telling me times are changing and a whole lot of other insights like war's bad, and people don't love each other, and the rich screw the poor, and communication's shot to hell. What a discerning cat, oh *man*. Put on some music, will you?"

"How about Miles?"

"Not Miles. Mozart."

VI

Behold the fire and the wood:
but where is the lamb?

π I took him to the zoo and he rode the burros, rode the
train, rode the merry-go-round. We saw monkeys and
snakes and crocodiles and gaudy painted birds; lions, tigers, elephants, polar bears. For me it was the D.T.'s but
he loved it all. I helped him to catch a brass ring on the
merry-go-round and bought him one of those balloons inside a balloon, fed him ice cream and popcorn and peanuts and a dust mop of pink cotton candy. I held his head
on the way home while he threw up in the weeds.

"Don't tell Mommy."

"It's our secret, chum."

It is our secret. Let us bow our heads and pray. The
hour is near at hand. *O Eternal God, who alone spreadest
out the heavens, and rulest the raging of the sea; we commend to thy almighty protection thy servant, for whose*

preservation on the great deep our prayers are desired.
Guard him, we beseech thee, from the dangers of the sea,
from the violence of his worthless father, and from every
evil to which he may be exposed in the company of the
degenerate and the hopeless. Let us bow our heads and
pray for the reversal of time and tide.

Ellen was pleased about the zoo. She even made that
soufflé, though I wasn't particularly hungry, and when I
asked to take him to Big Sur for the Thanksgiving weekend, she readily consented. She would not go herself.
Probably she had a heavy date with her philosopher and
was planning activities at which a little boy would be *de*
trop. In fact, I see now that she *used* me, and when you
use me, kiddo, you take potluck. I didn't guarantee to
walk him around on a leash. What am I? The owner of
the spheres that I should know all, see all? In my dreams
you point an accusing finger and cry "murderer" but it is
you, passive mother, that should be pointed at, not I. You
should have been there. I begged you to go, begged you.
And I heard that it was not yet time to try again. Old
wounds should heal before new ones are inflicted. You
were wrong, you see. New wounds have made corpses of
us all.

My dreams are waking dreams. Cineramic. Stereophonic.
More real than real because they are not altered by imagination. No grotesque figures, no fragmented sequences, no
unresolved endings where I wake up just as the guillotine
starts to fall. In my dreams it falls. Its razor edge slices
my head from my trunk and I drop into the basket with
open, staring eyes, and I go *on* dreaming. My dreams are
re-creations, and they are always the same.

There is a yellow Ford rattling down the highway through the Santa Clara Valley. Inside there are three adults, a boy, and an Airedale. The floor is littered with Cheese Nips, Baby Ruth wrappers, an empty bottle of Pernod, half a turkey sandwich wrapped in a Baggie, and Gina Pope's tights, which she has removed en route. The trunk of the car is packed with heavy coats, sleeping bags, blankets, a record player, a bundle of records, and a small suitcase that contains a pair of boy's pajamas, slippers, toothbrush and paste, a copy of *The Five Hundred Hats of Bartholomew Cubbins,* and a green squirt gun.

Gina is recounting the hour of her conversion. Through mescaline she has come to Christ. She has discovered God in all the things of this world. Most particularly in the oak tree outside her apartment window. "Face, form, and all," she says. "Man, even his privates. Right there in that tree which I mean I looked at a hundred times and never dug at all before. But this time I saw that me and it were part of the ONE, you know? Like it all fit into a groovy pattern and I was with it, I was IDENTIFIED. I really flipped. I dug the tree like one of those Indian mystic cats which are also hung up on nature. I was making a religious scene. . . . Oh WOW. . . . And dig, what's cool is it changed my whole life. I'm a different person. I am, really. I'm a very different person. I'm turned on to *people.* I *understand* them, I love them. . . . I guess after an epoxy you just can't be the same anymore."

"Epiphany," Gordon mutters.

"Yeah, right, epiphany."

They are rolling through the farming country below San Jose, through a broad plain between the Diablo Range and the Santa Cruz Mountains where the land is still orchards and long cultivated fields of produce, through Morgan Hill with its run-down stores, shabby streets, and loafing groups of itinerant farm workers who have not yet followed the season south to the San Bernardino and Imperial valleys. The highway is dotted with produce shacks and truck farmers parked along the shoulder; cider stands, orange juice stands, fresh lemonade stands, walnuts, peppers, honey products. "When are we going to get there, Dad?" the boy asks.

"Not for a couple hours. Relax."

At San Martin they stop at a winery offering tours and samples: go inside to check out the local varieties. Lousy wine, but free. A dapper-looking Italian boy in a red brocade vest serves them and begins his memorized spiel. "You are now tasting our world renowned Pinot Noir, made from the famous grape that yields the most best of the red burgundies that comes from France. It is smooth and velvet to the taste and its aroma is delightful to your palates." Pause. Seem to have garbled that one. Start again. "It is served to red meat, cheese, and birds . . . game, that is, in Engliss." Flashes a snowy grin. "Now I move you on to a different taste treat, our world-famous Grignolino. You can't get this fine wine in noplace but the Santa Clara Valley. It is native."

"Hey man," Gina interrupts him. "You got any Ripple or Thunderbird, or like that?"

The Italian eyes her. "No, lady, we do not artificial sweeten or carbonate our wines."

Gina makes a face. "Hey you guys, let's blow. I'm getting tired."

"You'll have to excuse the lady," Gordon says, hustling her off the stool and shoving her toward the door. "She just got epoxied to the oversoul. A bad trip. Bound in the molecular grasp of Himself—a captive audience, as it were." He pushes her out of the wine room and calls back to the brocade vest. "Thanks for the vinegar, dad. Your Pinot would go great on a tossed salad."

At Gilroy they stop in a supermarket for a six-pack of beer and Gina's Ripple. The boy is tired and looking as if he may cry and Ryan buys him an orange beach ball and a Pepsi. For the fifth time he answers his question, "A couple hours. We'll get there, relax. We'll have us a game of catch before supper." And as they are again under way, "Gimme a beer, Gordon."

"What the hell! You got Ripple in one hand, now you want beer in the other. Sober and with both hands you couldn't drive straight if Stirling Moss was here to help you." He hands the beer across and Ryan clamps it between his legs. "Whyn'cha sideswipe that cop car parked up at the stop sign?"

By five o'clock they wobble into Carmel and stop for more beer. Gordon buys a salami and a wedge of cheese and as they head south along the winding highway toward the Big Sur country they eat. The sun, low on the horizon, sets fire to the sweeping ridges and sheer cliffs that plunge into the sea-beaten coast. There is a path of diamonds across the water that spreads in an ever widening V out toward the flaming horizon, and behind, inland, the Santa Lucia Mountains blaze at the sundown with a golden fierceness that is born of another world.

"Robinson Jeffers country," says Gordon, and plays the poet.

"The beauty of things is in the beholder's brain—the human mind's translation of their transhuman intrinsic value."

"Jesus, you guys. I'm zonked out of my gourd," says Gina.

The sun drops to the edge of the sea, glows a moment like hot slag, and sinks beneath the water. As they round a curve the Point Sur ridges stretch off in a purple haze—folds in a crumpled blanket, furrowed hills of laurel and chaparral. Too rich a painting for any artist. Only a camera could catch this twilight, and even then one would swear it lied.

Gordon's window is open and he leans out, still quoting Robinson Jeffers, shouting against the wind that tears at his face.

> "The ebb slips from the rock, the shrunken
> Tide-rocks life streaming shoulders
> Out of the slack, the slow west
> Sombering its torch; a ship's light
> Shows faintly, far out,
> Over the weight of the prone ocean
> On the low cloud.
> Over the dark mountain, over the dark pinewood,
> Down the long dark valley along the shrunken river—

". . . something something something something. I forget the rest."

"Hey, I think I'm gonna get sick, you guys," says Gina, and slumps lower in her seat. "I'm juiced."

The dog growls in the back seat, tired of being hugged by the boy. The boy is exhausted and bored. He fidgets, asks again how long it will be until they get there, and is told to shut up. He begins to whimper and is once more told to shut up, to be a man. "You said we'd play ball," he whines. "And now it will be too dark."

"We'll play tomorrow. Hey, what do you like best in the world for breakfast?" Cheer him up. Be a sport.

The boy thinks a moment. "Waffles."

"Okay, buddy. You're on. Waffles it is. All you can eat and a gallon of syrup. Now hush up. We're almost there."

Over the dark mountain. Over the dark pinewood. When they reach the lodge below Pfeiffer State Park it is night and a soft mist makes halos around the porch lamps. They go into the bar where Gunboat and three or four others are arguing about contemporary theater. Candlelight and a half empty magnum of Rosé. Huge redwood puncheon on wrought-iron legs. Chairs of twisted steel rods with flat stone seats. They are attended by a black-haired barmaid named Dasha who eyes Ryan with familiar frankness. Not disconcerting enough. "Here's an old friend of Mike's," Gunboat says, taking her arm.

"I know. We've met." He bows. She smiles. "I'd like the key to the cabin. The boy is tired."

"There's sort of a party going on in there," Gunboat says. "You want to put him down in the other cabin? Or in the car?"

"I'll move the party out."

"The key's up there," says Dasha. "See you a little later?"

On the steps that lead up the hill to the double row of cabins a young man is sitting. He is bearded and wears his hair at shoulder length. His thumbs are hooked in the straps of his bib overalls. His mouth is slack and he stares vacantly out into the blackness.

"Hi," says the boy, as they walk up toward him.

There is no response until they are almost past. Then the

young man says dreamily, "High." He seems to taste the word, roll it around on his tongue for a moment. Then he tries a few variations. "High? . . . HIGH! . . . Hiiiiieeeee. . . ." Holds his nose. "I certainly am."

The boy is in bed. The party has moved to the other cabin, but its odor of wine and smoke lingers in the room and he wishes that he were at home with his mother sleeping across the hall. He thinks about Bartholomew Cubbins and he wonders how so many hats could fit on one head and why the King was angry when Bartholomew couldn't take them off. Five hundred hats. It couldn't happen. Maybe it *could* happen. Probably not, but maybe. Remember your old Aunt Effie. He hears shouting down by the lodge and the sound of a ball being kicked. The door opens cautiously and a head, my head, peers in. "You okay, bub?"

"Yes, Dad. Do they have my ball?"

"Yes. I'll see that it gets back in the car. They're just horsing around with it. Go to sleep now. I'll see you in the morning."

"Good night."

The door closes, then opens again. "Hey."

"Yes?"

"What's for breakfast?"

"Waffles," whispers the boy, but somehow he is not looking forward to them.

I had a son once, and his name was Sonny and he fell over the western edge of the land into the sea and I could not find him. At first I did not know. I thought he slept as I struggled with my nightmare . . . with my dream witch

. . . on sands made red by passing moons . . . on sands made slippery with leaves of blue lotus . . . on sands that move like cloth off a weaver's loom. And when I knew I ran. Through fields of oat and poppy, through fog and smog, through deserted streets of towns grown old, through tide pools of wind-whipped foam, until I came at last to the end of night where I saw my naked soul dance on a bed of white hot coals.

And still I ran. And still I run. From gulf to gulf I chase the vaporous dreams that swirl and vanish like a summer's dust. I am pierced by rays of light from the four corners of the earth. I am raw nerves and the agony of remembrance. I am the shadow of darkness—lost, deserted, and void.

Epilogue

π My masks are unlimited: my souls, infinite. I'm Alec Guinness playing seven parts in a single film; playing a single part in seven films; playing seven parts in seven films. I'm a cactus thorn needle caught in the defective groove of a long-playing record of defection. *Froggy went a-courting and he did ride, did ride, did ride, did ride, did ride, did ride.* I'm judge and jury, plaintiff and defendant, priest and executioner, strutting about in the clutter of my private theater. I'm set designer, stage manager, choreographer, cameraman. Produced and directed by . . . music and lyrics by . . . adapted from a novel by . . . and when it is over and everybody has gone home I wander down the aisles with my broom and sweep pan, cleaning up the popcorn and candy wrappers and cigarette butts. I fold back the seats and dim the houselights; rewind the film and thread the next feature through the projector. What will it be? Comedy? Tragedy? One of those grim, dark

243

tales with night sea journeys through storm and fire and plague? A sad-faced knight playing a game of chess with the devil's avatar on a lonely, smoky, blasted beach? Shall I run a few feet on the screen and peek into the future before it is swallowed by the past?

I see a field of orange poppies along the edge of the sea. A ragged coast all green through an early morning mist. Rocks out beyond the surf like the teeth of a medieval monster, mossy green, washed with foam, decayed. A small boy stands in the center of the field tossing an orange beach ball against the pale sky. He catches it, boots it high into the air, runs through the wild flowers after it. Closer to the edge now. A weathered fence of cedar posts teeters along the rim of the headland, totters over the brink of an eroded precipice, falls into the sea.

Enough. Rewind. I will see it all tomorrow and tomorrow and tomorrow. I will see it and see it and see it in the daily rebirth of yesterday. My private crucifixion and resurrection. Turn out the stage lights and go back into the dressing room for a last cup of coffee before bed; back into my room of mirrors.

Who is there? That shadow face in the glass? What is it you want? I'm closed. The show is over for tonight and I'm not up to another performance. Not for you. Especially not for you. Why is it you come along now when it's late and I'm tired and want to sleep? I've given in, admitted defeat. Why do you hound me, chase me around and around in the same black rut? Must we persist in this interminable interview, forever going over the same ground, covering the same points, probing the same wounds? I've thrown in the sponge. Uncle. King's X . . . seven, eight, nine, ten, RED LIGHT. I moved. I'm out of the game. I hear my mother calling from beyond the seawall, calling supper, and I'm running so deep in the sand that I'll be too late and I'll have to eat in the dusky kitchen by myself. You are not invited. I can't even remember anymore where you came from. Out of a sand-polished bottle washed up on some desolate beach? Out of a book? Out of the fantasy world of the university during some eye-strained, weary-minded bout with mystics and prophets from a fictional past? Out of Kubla's dome? Have I fed on honeydew and drunk the milk of an artist's paradise? Madness is divinity and creation.

Or was it out of some drugged afternoon? Out of a cactus, mushroom, weed that I smoked, ate, sniffed. When did I open my mouth and admit you into the antechamber of my mind? Trip along the red carpet, swing on a tonsil, float up into my skull and start splitting cells, breaking up molecules, tearing up memory and reason and scattering the bits and pieces like confetti until my brain looks like Coney Island after a Labor Day weekend. Your breath reeks of fish. Tang of salt in the air and I hear the cry of gulls as they circle over the tide pools in search of crabs that scuttle across the rocks and duck into the crevices. Did you crawl out of the sea? Some primitive mutation with gills still open on your throat like our baby when he was born? Did you lie in fetal slumber on the floor of a distant ocean, floating, when the time was near, along an undersea current to the dark red beach near Point Sur where a deadbeat dropout danced his crazy, drugged dance with a midnight witch? I hear suffering and pain and perversity. I hear the sea washing the unquiet grave of a small boy. In his mother's belly he kept warm and dark. I wonder how he keeps now.

Mirror, mirror, on the wall . . . why in God's name do

they hang mirrors in bathrooms, bedrooms, hallways, dressing rooms? . . . For actors? Yes. That's all right for an actor. He can look at himself in a mirror, but a human being . . . a human being begins to squirm and monkeyshine, gets embarrassed. An actor . . . he is not responsible for the clown's face. His reflection is only imagination. Milton? Mole, is that you? Is it really you? I had expected . . . no matter. Good to have you. Really, very good. We'll have a party. There are others here, you know, others, around, we'll have a party. Bring on the emperor of ice cream. I've just been talking with Fisher King whom I've known . . . God knows how long. Lot of water has flown under the bridge, hey Fish. The emperor here is in good humor, ha, ha, been north to Alaska tacking up mirrors in the primitives' privies in the land of the midnight bun, the chapped frosty little buns of midnight primitives in the private privies of the ethnic arctic. Good Christ, Mole, I swear to you, *I swear*, that it was not my fault.

Nobody believes. Excuses, pretexts, justifications, vindications. Nobody believes. Why must I play all the parts? Why must I be both accused and accuser? And how absurd to be found guilty. An actor is not responsible for his words, his actions; only his performance.

When did I start to go mad? From under what rock did I drag this apparition of my irresponsible soul? On a midsummer day on the broiling sand of the cove Ellen wandered through the afternoon and sliced her foot on a broken bottle. First link in the chain. Ellen's fault, not mine. If she had been watching where she was going I would not have met her, would not have pushed her on you, Mole, would not have taken her from you, Mole. There would have been no birth, no death; no hating, no guilt, no torturing. It was Ellen who began it all, Mole. I accuse Ellen, since she could never accuse me. You have to understand, old buddy, she was always taking her anger out of the room, suffering with lowered eyes like some squaw who deserved the crap that was being flung at her. Pariah. Bitch. Why couldn't you tell me to shut my face, to take my insufferable needling and take a flying leap in the bay? She was a subtle strategist, Mole. The kind of woman who goes on loving, sweetly, letting you hang yourself with your doubts, letting you go on testing, probing, questioning how much love can endure before the cable snaps and you fall on your ridiculous behind and sit there sucking your thumb and wondering where everyone has gone.

That won't really do, will it? Nobody believes. The lady may stand down, acquitted, the evidence is circumstantial and inadmissible.

Well, gentlemen of the jury—mirrors on the wall—what now? Where do we go from here? Another picture show? All we have is old movies. Reruns. If you insist I'll give you a sneak preview of tomorrow night's cartoon. *Neurosis and Psychosis: Mickey Mouse Takes a Swim.* Perhaps we will discover in it the origins of certain behavioral patterns that we have been considering. Perhaps not. Take a seat here on the aisle, Mole, it's more comfortable and you can stretch your legs.

A lake, blue as the eye of God, nestled in a shallow bowl in the Green Mountains, fringed around with pine, cedar, chokecherry, blueberry. Back in time. Before time. Before California, where nothing begins. Back from the shore, summer cottages with screened porches and steps that lead down to the water; dinner bells that call before-lunch swimmers from the rocks and floats. Sandwiches and ice tea with fruit juice and a nap from one to three, and in my room I would sometimes wake up and go on dreaming, hear my mother calling from downstairs as I run through knee-deep sand in a slow-motion attempt to escape from sleep.

In the sky there are little explosions of cloud, drifted smoke from the artillery barrage that booms off in the distance. Osiris and Typhon warring behind the hump of Mount Mansfield. Christ's legions trumpeting an end to the Prince of Darkness. When Satan falls he falls into my dream and chases me through the sand, and I wake to the sound of rain on the shingles and the boom of thunder over the lake and my mother calling downstairs. When the storm blows past, the earth assaults my nose; cedar spice and fern musk, the faint sweetness of wild strawberry, clover, and mown hay. The steam that rises from the porch logs is heavy with creosote and everywhere there is a piney-wood sachet of wet needles and rotten logs.

On the dock below a white framed cottage there are three or four late afternoon swimmers: a young woman in a blue bathing suit, two men wearing trunks that look like woolen jockey shorts, held up by white belts with metal buckles. In the water, just off the end of the dock, a boy, maybe four or five years old, dog-paddles around with a pair of water wings under his armpits, and near him a black Labrador swims circles around a wood chip that one of the men has thrown for him. When the dog snaps at the chip it washes just out of reach in front of his nose.

The woman is stretched out on a striped bath towel and the men sit with their feet dangling off the dock, smoking, encouraging the dog. After a bit, one of them flips his